ALSO BY THOMAS PRIDE

King and Country

Mercia

The Baron

Wonderful Untouchables

Zayed

Fever

THOMAS PRIDE

Ucadia Books Company

Published by Ucadia Books Company, a Delaware stock corporation (File Number 6779670) 901 N Market St #705 Wilmington Delaware 19801.
First edition.

Thomas Pride is the pen name and true ancestor of an Australian based philosopher and writer.

ISBN 978-1-64419-000-5

Northern Australia

Few places in the world remain as untamed and unforgiving as Northern Australia. If the extreme heat or dangerous floods do not get to you, then there is arguably the largest collection of deadly insects and animals in any one place on Earth.

Northern Australia is also one of the last great potential resources for immense mineral wealth, including gold and precious gems. But during the wet season, whole towns and valleys can be cut off by the flood waters for weeks at a time.

So imagine what could happen if, during the wet season, a small town experienced a sudden and dramatic gold rush, only then to be "cut off" from modern civilisation for a period of time?

Imagine then if not all the people who are newly arrived are what they appear?

To Katie.

If patience is worth anything, it must endure to the end of time. And a living faith will last in the midst of the blackest storm.

Mahatma Gandhi

Chapter 1

Tightly spaced ridges on the unsealed road caused the vibration coursing through the 4WD to have an oddly melodic tone. Fingers reached down to the central console to skip a tune on the stereo system. Then another and another, until the pretty young female driver (Lisa Riordin) started to hum and then sing to a song. Not awful, but not great.

Outside, the familiar desolation of the classic Australian Outback; endless spinefex, gripping fire red earth, occasionally punctuated by giant termite mounds, with a cloud of red dust coating and trailing the vehicle.

Just before the repeat of the chorus, the sound of a blessedly ridiculous phone ring tone interrupted her singing. She reached across and turned down the volume of the stereo before pressing a phone button located on the steering wheel.

"Hello Lisa?" The American voice (Elisa) sounded hesitant given the background noise of the melodic drone of the vehicle vibration.

"Hi mom," she replied in a less obvious accent.

"I can hardly hear you. Where are you? Your stepfather and I -"

Fever

"I'm fine mom. I'm driving."

"What? Did you say you are OK? Are you sure honey, because I can fly over and see you while Bruce minds the puppies and -"

A deep sigh from Lisa, before she shouted back, "Mom, seriously I am fine, I just -"

The phone Beeped twice signalling new messages.

"He seemed such a perfect match; and now with all the costs of cancelling the preparations, I thought - "

"Mom, I can't talk about it right now."

"What was that honey, you -"

"I can't talk right now."

"Oh, OK, I lov -"

Lisa hung up the call. Another deep sigh, before she pressed the phone button on the steering wheel again. Two new messages. She let them play, hearing a distinct but stuttering male Australian voice (Kieran).

"Hey, its me. You haven't returned any of my messages, so I called your office and they said you have left on some kind of assignment up north. Anyway, I just wanted to apologize again for my stupid behaviour, and ah-"

Lisa punched the button interrupting the playback. The voice mail signalled the second of two messages. "I love you still, and ah -"

Chapter 1

Lisa punched the button again, cutting off the message as the playback signalled the end of messages.

"Arsehole!" she muttered, before flicking the volume on the stereo to maximum.

****

On the same dusty unsealed road, a few hundred miles behind, a new model Range Rover weaved its way along. Dark and heavy storm clouds hugged the horizon. The older driver (Ken) looked over at his companion (Dorothy) as she stared blankly out at the barren red landscape. Cheesy 1980's elevator style music played in the car cabin. He reached down to the central console and started to fiddle with the air conditioning dials.

Zero, then six. Clear frustration rising on a simple task. He redoubled his concentration on the dials and in that moment, the car wobbled violently as he was distracted, causing Dorothy to snap her head around at him to see what he was doing.

"Stop fiddling with it," she barked. "Just focus on the road."

His hand retreated back onto the wheel, as Dorothy let out a voluminous sigh, like a punctured beach ball.

Fever

"You said we would be there an hour ago."

Ken remained mute, feigning deafness. An awkward silence.

"Well? This will be the death of me," Dorothy moaned. Another awkward silence.

"You're the one who wanted to see the real Australia," Ken added sheepishly. "Have you called John to let him know we'll be late?"

Dorothy ignored him, shaking her head, before she turned away to pretend she was studying the monotonous scenery out the window. A moment later, Ken started to slow down the car.

"What is it?"

Just ahead, was the faint outline of a white vehicle on the side of the road coming into focus through the heat haze.

"What are you doing?" An air of nervousness in her voice.

"Someone's broken down."

Ken continued to slow down the car.

"For goodness sake Ken," she exclaimed insistently, "Don't stop."

Ken threw her a look of disdain.

Chapter 1

"Don't look at me like that," she said. "Well, they could be like that fellow. You know the Wolf Creek one."

"Dorothy, this is not Double Bay. I have to see if they're all right."

As they inched closer, the make of the car became clear - a white Ford station wagon slumped almost completely in the ditch. Reclined against the car was a handsome athletic looking man (Karl Ratzner), who made eye contact with Ken as he pulled up. Karl gave him a brief nod of appreciation before stubbing out a half finished cigarette.

Karl stepped over to the drivers side window of the Range Rover as Ken lowers the glass.

"You OK?" asks Ken.

"My car hit a Kangaroo," Karl smiles in reply.

Ken pulled the Range Rover onto the side of the road, just in front, keeping the engine running, before he unclipped his seat belt to get out. Dorothy projected one final expression of horror at the gesture of good will. Ken then stepped over to the front of the vehicle in the ditch where Karl was now standing. Bits of meat and fur are still stuck to the bull bar with hundreds of flies swarming around. Ken quickly covered his nose and mouth with his hand because of the stench.

Fever

"I don't think you're going anywhere in this," Ken muttered before covering his nose and mouth again and gasping.

Karl smiled warmly, seemingly non-fazed by the smell. "Yes. One minute I was driving and the next minute this giant Kangaroo was right in front of my car."

Ken nodded back, while he still covered his nose and mouth, before taking a few steps back and far enough away from the smell to put his hand down. "American right?"

"On a driving holiday of this beautiful land of yours," Karl replied.

Ken looked over at Dorothy still sitting in the passengers seat with the feign appearance of calm and starts mouthing over to her 'American'. She shrugged her shoulders. Ken shouts at her direction.

"He's an American. A tourist."

Dorothy shook her head as if to say she didn't understand, or didn't want to understand. Ken then turned back to Karl.

"Well, we can give you a lift to the next town to get help."

"Thank you," Karl responded and patted Ken on the arm. "I'll just get my things."

Chapter 1

Karl turned and walked to the back of the broken station wagon, as Ken followed.

"I'll give you a hand," Ken chimed.

Karl was already at the back of station wagon with the rear door open as Ken inched closer.

"The wife was worried. She didn't want me to stop. You know all the stories..."

As Ken continued to speak, the contents of the back of the station wagon were revealed. Two army green duffel bags and a few tools, including a shovel. Karl briefly unzips one of the bags exposing for a moment the butt of a rifle.

As Ken moved alongside, Karl tilted his head to him "Yes. You can never be too careful."

****

The storm clouds that were on the horizon had inched their way closer as the Range Rover from earlier barrelled down the road at high speed. The same cheesy music playing. Except, Ken was not driving. Karl was driving, while humming to the same terrible music and smoking a cigarette. Ken and Dorothy nowhere to be seen.

Fever

Chapter 2

Lisa slowed down the 4WD on approach to a sign saying *Warratama - Historic Goldmining Town - Population 1,000*. She allowed herself a wry smile at the sight of someone having partly obscured the number by adding the word *dead* at the end of the sign.

A few yards further along, the road took a dog leg across a rickety bridge over a dry creek bed. On the other side of the bridge, the town of Warratama finally came into view - a few dozen run down buildings, a handful of cars and not a living soul in sight.

She pulled the 4WD up outside a weathered and forlorn outback timber building. A classic verandah hugging its front facade. The only clue as to its purpose, a cracked old style police light out the front, above a broken gate and fencing. Next to where she had parked her vehicle was an old dust covered police utility truck, that had seen better days. As she got out, the word POLICE on the side of her vehicle was revealed and that Lisa herself was wearing a short sleeve Western Australian police constable uniform.

Lisa briefly looked up at the approaching storm clouds almost overhead. The daylight had turned into an eerie twilight, contrasting with the blood red earth.

Yet still no sign of life around. She shut the cabin door of her vehicle and walked over to the front door of the station, covered by an old wire fly-screen.

She pulled back the wire fly-screen and turned the front door knob. It was locked.

"Great," she mumbled sarcastically to herself.

She pressed an old and dirty buzzer next to the front door, then counted to three. Nothing. She tried again, counting to ten, and then once more. Still no answer.

"Just perfect."

Lisa stepped off the verandah and looked down the side of the station toward an open gate. She walked through it and to the back of the station, where she found the back door unlocked. She opened the door and went inside, to find herself standing in a stale 1950's style kitchen - the only modern accessory being a sexist calendar hung prominently on the fridge.

Cautiously, she proceeded along a hallway connecting from the kitchen. The first door she tried was locked, so Lisa moved to the second door along, to find it slightly ajar. She pushed it open a little further to reveal an older man (Senior Sergeant Mitch Rory) lying on a single bed in his pants and singlet, with his back to the door. The singlet only partly hiding an array of scars across his back and left shoulder. Lisa stepped inside the room as quietly as possible, moving closer to the resting officer. A squeaky floorboard alerted Mitch to the presence of someone else in the room. Before she could say anything, Mitch swung around on the bed, holding a gun pointed at her head. She jumped back in fright.

"Holy crap," she yelled.

Mitch at first seemed to struggle to get his focus and spot the police uniform of Lisa, while she remained frozen at the sight of the gun pointed at her.

"You're not Marjory," he grunted. Slowly he withdrew the gun and set it down on the side table.

An audible sigh from Lisa. "You scared the hell out me."

Mitch rolled over and out of bed. He shoved past Lisa to retrieve a police sergeant shirt hanging on the back of the door, pushing her out of the room.

"One minute. A bit of privacy," he snapped, before slamming the door on her abruptly.

"Who is Marjory?" asked Lisa. No answer. She waited then tried again. "I'm Constable Lisa Riordin from Perth. Your request for support. You remember?" Still no answer. "Look, I am sorry if I…"

The door to the room flung open revealing a fully clothed Mitch, who proceeded to march straight past Lisa and toward a door at the far end of the corridor. Lisa scurried after him.

"Sergeant, I apologise if I startled you."

Lisa followed him into the main part of the station, an open room, dominated by a front counter, separating a waiting area, then an office area of several spare desks and one main desk obscured by paper. In the corner was a set of classic iron bar cells. Lisa watched as Mitch shuffled underneath a pile of papers, retrieving a set of keys.

Mitch lifted a hatch in the front counter, stepping into the public area and moved to the front door, unlocking it. As he turned, for the first time, he looked directly at Lisa.

"You're a creeper. I hate creepers," he snarled, before returning to the desk drowning in paper to retrieve a set of reading glasses.

"But the front door was locked. You just unlocked it," she protested.

"An American," he mumbled.

"Yes, I am an American," she replied. "But my father was Australian. So, as I was saying let's start again, I -"

Chapter 2

At that moment, the wire fly-screen door to the station swung open and two men barrelled in: the first a sweaty middle aged Asian man (Barry) in dirty mechanics overalls with Barry's Fine Motors on the back; the second an Indian looking man (Antonio) in a bow tie and old clothes.

"This man is a thief. Arrest him Mitch," yelled Antonio.

"Bullshit. I did exactly what you asked me to do."

"You are a fraud Barry," screamed Antonio in reply.

Mitch ignored both men as he finished scribbling on a piece of paper, folding it into his top pocket, then flicking his glasses onto the table.

"On everything that is sacred, I swear he destroyed my car."

"Rubbish. Rubbish. Rubbish," replied Barry

Mitch got up and headed to the hatch, to get through the counter to the front door. Lisa followed him.

"Sergeant," she protested. "The email from the assistant commissioner's office. You sent a request."

Mitch ignored her and instead turned to Antonio. "Antonio, can't help you mate." Then he turned to Barry. "Cut him some slack Barry."

Mitch flung open the wire fly-screen door. "Can't speak. Got to see the Doc," he said, before stepping outside. Lisa leapt after him.

Outside, Mitch looked up at the approaching storm clouds before striding over to the old police utility vehicle, with Lisa following him. He opened the driver's side passenger door and retrieved a rain jacket and hat from the back seat and then opened the driver's door. Lisa remained silent, looking slightly sorrowful as she stood in front of the old truck.

Mitch paused for a moment at the sight of Lisa and then sighed. He then waved his hand for her to get in and started up the truck, throwing it into reverse, just as Lisa managed to get into the passenger side seat and close the door.

Mitch swung the police utility vehicle around and out onto the main street of Warratama.

"Where are we going?" she asked politely.

No sooner had she asked, than Mitch slowed down, stopped the truck and parked it out the front of a store with the sign *Warratama Veterinary Hospital*, just two hundred yards from the police station.

"We could have walked" she said light-heartedly, as Mitch got out of the cabin and headed to the door of the Veterinary Surgery. "Do you want me to lock the truck?" she yelled as Mitch stepped inside, ignoring her. She slapped her forehead and sighed. "Of course he doesn't dumb ass," she said to herself. "It's the frigging outback."

****

Inside the Veterinary Surgery was a main waiting room and reception, full of outback characters and their pets - the pets looking relatively normal. Sitting in-between the pets and their owners was a small girl with her arm bandaged and an older farmer wearing a neck brace. As Lisa stepped inside, a matronly looking woman (Marjory), sitting behind a reception desk, looked up and smiled at her.

"Hello, I'm Marjory."

"Lisa, Lisa Riordin," Lisa smiled back.

Marjory signalled for Lisa to go through a door marked surgery. "Mitch is inside with Doc."

Lisa nodded appreciatively and walked over to the surgery door.

Inside the Vet surgery, Mitch was standing next to a taller older man (Doc) watching him finish the final stitches to the leg of a young boy, with the mother of the boy watching nervously.

Fever

"And that is why God gave you a spare, son," the Doc chuckled.

Both the Doc and Mitch looked up as Lisa walked into the surgery, before the Doc re-focused on finishing his stitching on the boys leg.

"There. All done," smiled Doc, as the boy sprung off the table and ran out of the surgery. "And don't pull those stitches," he yelled after the boy.

"Thanks Mitch," the mother said, shaking his still rubber gloved hands, before the mother smiled at Lisa and then turned and exited to chase after her boy.

Doc pulled off the gloves and threw them in a bin next to the operating table and reached over, to shake the hand of Lisa.

"Hi I'm Doc."

"Lisa Riordin, from Perth," she smiled.

Mitch made eye contact with the Doc before rolling his own eyes. "My new assistant from Perth.

The Doc shook his head as a young girl with a terrier entered into the surgery.

"You'll have to forgive Mitch," the Doc said to Lisa. "He may be a bit rough on the outside, but really he is harmless."

"Speak for yourself Doc," grumbled Mitch in reply as the Doc started laughing.

Chapter 2

Looking at the dog now on the table, the Doc said, "And what have you swallowed this time Scruffy?"

Doc started putting on new rubber gloves as the young girl continued to calmly pat Scruffy on the table.

"You're going to be busy Doc," said Mitch. "The rain has come early."

Doc sighed as he stuck a rubber glove covered hand up the backside of the dog, causing Scruffy to yelp.

"Sorry Scruffy. This is the price you pay for swallowing crap."

Lisa looked over at the Doc and then at Mitch. "What do you mean by busy?" she asked.

"Doc here is our local miracle worker," said Mitch. "Warratama doesn't have a GP. Hasn't had one for more than twenty years," he continued.

Doc finished looking at the backside of the dog and discarded the rubber gloves, signalling for the girl take him off the table. "It seems ghosts and ghost towns don't need doctors," replied Doc. "So any breaks, cuts or bruises they come to me. And when it rains, all the cockies and station hands come into the Grand Hotel, to celebrate -"

"And just in case the town is flooded in," Mitch added, before slapping Doc on the back. "Anyway Doc, just popped in to let you know that thing is sorted."

An audible sigh of relief from the Doc. "Thank goodness for people like you Mitch and the strings you pulled."

Mitch turned and reached for the surgery door. "So stop worrying," said Mitch as he opened the door. "But no more pulling out appendixes without notifying Perth OK. Otherwise next time, I won't be able to help."

****

As steady drops of rain turned the dust on the windscreen into streaks of mud, Karl continued to drive the Range Rover at high speed along the unsealed highway. His mobile phone began to ring, so he put it on speaker.

"Ratzner."

"You didn't call," said the voice.

"Nothing to worry about," replied Karl. "Catching up now."

The source and location of the voice was revealed. On a fishing trawler in rolling seas, somewhere off the coast, a blond haired man (Peter) was holding onto the railing next to the wheel house.

Chapter 2

"We will be there to pick you up in two days," Peter replied.

"How are the kids?" Karl asked.

Peter started to walk with the phone to the back of the boat and an opening to the storage holds below. Peter looked down at another man (Gunther) securing boxes of crates, with one half open. Inside were guns neatly stacked in wrapping paper.

"Yes. Fine. All good," he smiled.

As visibility continued to worsen with the steady increase in rain, Karl eased back on speed and flicked the wind shield wipers to maximum.

"See you Sunday then."

Karl hung up the phone and started to dial another number. Just then a Ute screamed past tooting its horn, almost colliding with the Range Rover.

As the car pulled in front of the Range Rover, a young long haired hoon stuck his head out of the passenger window yelling profanities, a large rock spinning up from the back tyres of the Ute hitting and then smashing the windscreen of the Range Rover.

"SHIT."

Karl grappled with the steering wheel as the Range Rover swerved toward the side of the road. Karl put his foot on the brake peddle, the windscreen a shattered and muddy mess. Karl thumped his hands on the steering wheel in frustration.

"Shit."

Chapter 3

Sporatic droplets of rain had given way to a steady drizzle, as Mitch and Lisa stood in the middle of the highway, having to direct infrequent traffic. Nearby, a cattle truck was in the process of being pulled out by a tow truck from a side ditch. The driver of the cattle truck watched from the opposite side of the road.

"That should do it Reg," yelled Mitch to the driver of the tow truck, as the cattle truck lurched back onto the road surface.

An older Aboriginal man (Reg) stepped down from the cabin of the tow truck and approached Mitch and Lisa, while the driver of the now unstuck cattle truck shuffled across and started checking for any serious damage.

Reg stared at the figure of Mitch in his raincoat and hat and then at Lisa, wet to the bone.

"Lady you're soaked," he frowned at Lisa. "She'll get sick Mitch."

Mitch looked over at Lisa and shrugged his shoulders, causing her to cross her arms in a huff.

"I'm fine," she replied sarcastically. "Part of the job it seems."

"The creeks already flooded the local camp site," added Reg. "The mob have moved back to the larger camp over the gully. So won't be long before the town is cut off until the end of the rains."

The cattle truck driver stepped over to Mitch, Lisa and Reg.

"Thanks," the driver said sheepishly.

"Take it slowly next time," grumbled Mitch. "For now, just keep going. Otherwise, you'll be feeding those Cattle by hand yourself out the back stalls of the Grand for the next week or two."

The Cattle Truck driver nodded nervously to Mitch, before trotting back to his cattle truck and starting it up. Reg turned around and did the same.

As both men walk back to their trucks, Mitch looked over at Lisa, shivering and dripping wet.

"I suppose I better get you out of this weather," he said. "I'll take you to the Grand Hotel."

****

Mitch drove along the rain soaked main street of Warratama. One empty shop after another, except for a few odd signs of life like Antonios Tandoori Italian Restaurant.

Fever

"The Vet wasn't joking when he said it was a ghost town," smiled Lisa to no response.

Mitch stopped the police truck out in front of the Grand Hotel, next to a ute. The same ute seen with two youths who caused the breaking of the windscreen of the Range Rover driven by Karl.

Lisa pulled out her bags from the back seat and followed Mitch up and through the main door into the main reception.

Inside, the main foyer of the Grand Hotel resembled some faded exhibit of frontier gold rush hotels and whore houses. A clutter of dusty memorabilia and forgotten memories. As soon as Mitch and Lisa walked in, a large woman (Greta) rushed over from behind a colonial era reception desk to greet them.

"Thank god. Mitch, the Johnson boys are out of control," she protested.

Greta barely looked at Lisa until she noticed the pool of water coming from her soaked uniform.

"Mitch! She'll die of pneumonia!"

Mitch looked nonplussed at the rebuke, before Greta grabbed Lisa by the right arm and started to drag her in the direction of a grand staircase.

"Don't worry darling. We have a lovely suite for you," she said in a gentle voice, in contrast to the strength of her grip. "We'll get you out of these wet clothes in no time."

Lisa initially surrendered to allowing Greta to fuss over her. "Thank you," she replied.

"Ah an American!" declared Greta. "Greta. You can call me Greta. And what is your name darling?"

Lisa grimaced politely as she turned back to watch Mitch make himself scarce by exiting through a door labelled Grand Bar connected to the main hotel foyer. Lisa stopped walking, then turned, breaking the grip of Greta. "Lisa. My name is Lisa. But as you can see, I am a police woman and am perfectly fine."

Before Greta could re-attach her grip, Lisa had already made quick tracks after Mitch to the Grand Bar exit.

"Mitch will be fine. Don't let them scare you," shouted Greta. "I'll be here if there is anything you need."

Lisa walked through door connecting to the bar and as if into another era. The Grand Bar was full of smoke, noise, classic rock and roll music and a mix of characters. Mitch was talking to two scruffy looking older men (Greenhope) and (Cooper). In a corner furthest from the bar some young men with a couple of girls were clinking beers and shouting out the words of a song. They stopped singing when Lisa entered and instead started wolf whistling. Mitch turned to see the focus of wolf whistles being Lisa. He stepped over and put his left hand on the shoulder of Lisa.

"Why don't you get changed? With your wet uniform, some of the locals might get the wrong impression."

At first Lisa frowned at the insinuation of Mitch, until she looked down at her wet shirt, tightly hugging her chest.

"Right, yep. Bit embarrassing."

But as Lisa swung around to make a quick exit from the bar, her path was promptly blocked by Greenhope and Cooper, looking like two eager vultures, waiting to be fed. Mitch shook his head in dismay.

"Spook and Coop, this is a new one from Perth." Both men let out an 'ahh' as the wolf whistles from the back continued. Stupidly lecherous grins transfixed on their faces.

"No, she is a *real* cop."

Lisa narrowed her gaze at both men and then pointed to her service weapon. "With a *real* gun."

Chapter 3

Both men looked at one another then at Lisa, then at Mitch before bursting into hysterical laughter. Greenhope lifted his shirt, to reveal a revolver, followed by Cooper also carrying a side arm.

Instinctively, Lisa stepped back, turning her shoulder, feeling down for the button, to unclip her gun.

"What the -"

"Relax constable," interrupted Mitch, clearly seeing the worry on the face of Lisa. "It's the outback, constable."

Greenhope and Cooper also sensed the danger. "Yeah, not the city," said Greenhope.

"Snakes," added Cooper. "Snakes and crocs."

Lisa shook her head, relaxing her stance slightly.

"Yep big ones," said Greenhope. "And wild pigs and dogs."

Lisa raised her right elbow and nudged Greenhope out of the way.

"Whatever," she huffed. "Get out of my way, so I can leave."

Lisa charged to the door back to the hotel reception area as Mitch himself started to laugh. At the sound, she stopped and swung around, to give him a foul look.

Fever

"Get changed. Take your time," he chuckled. "I'll be here and when you get back. I'll shout you whatever is your poison."

Lisa flung open the door and stomped away.

****

A moment of soothing warmth and tranquillity in an old oversized style bath. Lisa closed her eyes, trying not to cough. She let the past few days wash over her. The trauma of the breakup with her fiancé Hartley. The embarrassment of how she felt around Mitch and the locals. The stress of the job and confrontation she ultimately came to do at Warratama. The deception of her ex-fiancé. The distant memories of her father.

Yes a moment of peace. Except, none of the thoughts that flooded through her mind made her feel very peaceful. How could there be any resolution to such still raw and open wounds? Sitting in the bath no longer felt tranquil, but uncomfortably overwhelming. So, she stepped out of the bath, dried herself and started to get dressed in civilian clothes.

Before leaving the room, Lisa checked her mobile phone. The bandwidth was sitting on one bar and 3G. She had two missed calls- one more from Kieran and one missed call from the Office of Assistant Police Commissioner James Miles.

****

The Range Rover inched to a halt outside the front of the Grand Hotel. Karl stepped out and noticed the same ute that caused him the damage parked next to the Police Truck. He walked around to the back of the Range Rover and pulled out his bags, but leaving a blanket partly covering a shovel. In the briefest of time that the back of the car remained exposed to the elements, the rain struck the tip of the shovel, causing hair and thick congealed drops of blood to flush away. He closed the back of the car and walked up to the main entrance of the hotel.

****

Lisa and Mitch, still in his police uniform, stood at the edge of the main bar in the Grand Lounge Bar of the hotel. The atmosphere had become even busier and rowdier. Yet the wolf whistles continued with less skill.

"Don't worry about them," said Mitch, as he looked over at the direction of the main source of the wolf whistles. "The Johnson boys are sometimes the only entertainment around here."

"Is this normal?"

"Not really," smiled Mitch, before taking a sip of his beer. "Bit slow. Come peak stock season, this bar used to be full. Since the bigger mines set up further west, most of the shops have closed down and few prospectors are left. All that's left are a few good people, a lot of empty shops and a few lowlifes."

"And the phone network is crap," added Lisa. "I had better reception on the highway."

"We only have an old mobile tower behind the hotel, next to the town generators," he replied. "On a good day, if the wind is right it can get up to 4G."

Lisa observed as a slippery looking man (Mayor Dick Masters) crept up behind Mitch, eyeballing her. He placed his hands on the shoulders of Mitch.

"Sorry to interrupt Mitch," interrupted Mayor Dick Masters, "but who is this ravishing beauty in our midst?"

Mitch swung around to see the beaming face of the Mayor as Lisa extended her hand to him.

"Lisa Riordin."

"Ah but an American?"grinned the Mayor, taking far too long to stop shaking her hand.

"My father was Australian," she replied, removing her hand.

"Ah a pretty police woman, just what this town needs. A new image."

Lisa smiled as politely as she could and looked over at Mitch, who secretly rolled his eyes, so she could see, but the Mayor could not.

"Dick here, is the local mayor," Mitch said dryly. "The head dick, if you will."

The barman (Andre) behind the main bar, had been listening in on the conversations. When he heard Mitch, he lost it and started laughing uncontrollably. The Mayor stared foully at Mitch, before he composed himself and whipped out a card and handed it to Lisa.

"Yes, I am the Mayor of Warratama," he said proudly.

"And the local real estate agent, landlord, conveyancer, notary and postmaster," added Mitch, while Andre the barman continued to struggle to regain control of his laughter.

"Yes, well Sergeant," frowned the Mayor, "to some falls great responsibility."

At that moment Karl walked through the door into the Grand Lounge. Lisa spotted him immediately, causing the Mayor to look over, as Karl walked toward Andre the barman.

Toward the back of the Main Bar, the Johnson boys also spotted Karl, and go strangely silent. Karl now eyes Lisa and smiled at her, before he tried to get the attention of Andre the barman.

"Excuse me," said Karl. He waited until Andre came over. "Could you please direct me to a repair shop in this town?"

"You're another yank?" replied Andre.

Karl looked at him strangely.

"Your wheels are playing up mate?" added Andre the barman.

"Excuse me?"

"Sorry mate," said Andre. "Didn't mean to confuse you. Your American right?"

Karl nodded while he looked around the room and noticed the Johnson boys from the ute that wrecked his windscreen seated at the back table drinking beers with others, staring at him. He was too busy glaring at them to notice Mitch next to him at the bar.

"Some hillbilly kids tried to run me off the road," said Karl as he continued to eyeball the Johnson brothers. "My windscreen was damaged."

"You said someone tried to run you off the road?"

Chapter 3

Karl turned around and was startled to see Mitch in his police sergeant uniform next to him. But before anyone got a word in, Mayor Dick interrupted.

"Sorry to interrupt Mitch," said the Mayor, "but I have matter of utmost importance to discuss."

Mitch ignored the Mayor and instead continued to look at Karl and then at the Johnson boys at the back table, looking more and more sheepish.

"Can you make out a description of the car or the driver?" asked Mitch.

"No, it is no problem officer," smiled Karl. "It was raining. I couldn't make out the pick up or who was driving. If I can just find a repair shop I can fix my windscreen and go."

Mitch shrugged his shoulders and looked back at the youths sitting at the back of the bar, frozen like mannequins.

"Barry over there," said Mitch pointing to Barry sitting down and having a beer with Antonio. The two of them were slapping each other on the back and laughing as if nothing had happened between them. "Barry is a magician with all types of engines and cars."

"He's the only mechanic in four hundred miles," added Andre the barman. "You can't miss his place."

Mayor Dick stepped forward, interrupting Mitch and Karl. "Mitch is it true you're going to close Lazy Creek and Gully Roads by the end of the week?"

"If this rain keeps up, said Mitch. "Then we'll have no option."

Mitch looked back at Karl. "Mate. I'd get your car fixed pretty quick," he grinned. "Otherwise, you'll be seeing a lot more of the Johnson boys and the other characters of this place."

Karl extended his hand to Mitch, who shook it. "Thanks for your help."

As he turned to walk away, for a brief moment Karl looked at Lisa and smiled, before heading for the exit. Mitch also watched Karl leave as Mayor Dick tapped Mitch on the shoulder.

"Mitch? Mitch? What about the investor meeting at the end of the week? If we're cut off then all that planning is down the drain."

Mitch grabbed his beer, took a big sip before looking at the Mayor. "Well Dick," grinned Mitch, "The ghosts will just have to keep us company for a few more months then."

****

Chapter 3

At Barry's Fine Motors, Barry was busily ripping off the windscreen of the Range Rover causing more glass to shatter. Karl was to the side with a phone to his ear. He glared at Barry because of the additional noise on top of the rain.

"Peter, a change in plans," yelled Karl into the phone. "I am stuck in a place called Warratama until the car is fixed."

"What about another car?" asked Peter over the phone.

Karl looked over at Barry, still pulling out the rubber seal from the front window of the car.

"No good," replied Karl. "It is too small a town. And the local police-"

He stopped speaking as Barry was tapping him on the shoulder. Karl swung around and glared at him.

"Hold on a moment," said Karl into the phone, cupping the speaker.

"You leave keys," said Barry. "Can't fix till glass comes. Going to take a couple of days-"

"I am on the phone," growled Karl.

"Two days," insisted Barry. "You give me the keys, I call you when ready."

Fever

Karl turned his back from Barry and removed his hand from the phone. "I have to wait," said Karl on the phone. "Two days at maximum. I will call you back."

Karl hung up the phone and reached into his pocket and produced the car keys, flinging them at Barry.

Chapter 3

Chapter 4

In the now solid rain, Mitch pulled up the old police truck at the entrance gate to a high fenced off mining area. A couple of fading warning signs, hanging either side of the gate. Over the other side of the fence line was a scarred moonscape dotted with mounds of tailings and bits of rusting mining equipment.

Mitch and Lisa stepped out of the truck. Lisa this time wearing rain protective gear over her police uniform.

"We'll walk from here," said Mitch. He watched as Lisa sneezed again. "You OK?"

"Fine," replied Lisa unconvincingly. "What is this place?"

"Fifteen years ago, a mining company claimed the rights to the old goldfields to process the old tailings, but went broke. About all that's left are the tailings, and old mines around this area. Old Albert Warner is about the last of his breed."

Mitch and Lisa walked along between tailing heaps to the front of a small cabin, festooned with all kinds of warnings and *Get Out* signs.

"Albert it's Mitch Rory," yelled Mitch. "We come in peace."

Fever

The door to the cabin creaked open and a shotgun peaked out. Lisa reached to unhinge her gun, before Mitch signalled for her to stop.

"Whoever you are, this is my property," screeched the voice. "Get away."

"Warner, It's Mitch. I've brought someone to see you."

The gun slowly withdrew back into the cabin. "I don't want to see anybody," the old voice coughed. "I am too busy. Go away."

"Albert it's a new police woman," added Mitch "She won't bite."

The door inched open and a hunched man with wispy grey hair (Albert Warner) emerged. His spectacles taped together and tied with rubber bands.

"A police vooman?" said Warner in a half interested tone.

He moved closer and surveyed Lisa, who was trying to stand despite occasionally coughing and sniffling.

"A police vooman eh?"

Warner smiled revealing rotting and missing teeth.

"I am showing her around," smiled Mitch. "I thought I might show her some local hospitality."

Chapter 4

"A police vooman," said Warner, now with a lecherous tone, causing Lisa to stomp her boots in the mud, sending water and dirt flying in all directions.

"What? What!" she protested, "I am not some kind of ornament," she coughed. "What is wrong with you men?"

Warner stumbled back looking bewildered at her outburst.

"Don't be offended," smiled Mitch. "Warner likes you. Normally he shoots people first. It's just that not too many attractive young woman live around these parts, especially a police VOOMAN."

Warner waved his hand negatively. "Ahgh, Captain Rory, she is too skinny to be a proper police vooman."

Lisa put her hands on her hips in disgust, before she turned to start walking back to the truck, interrupted by a giant sneeze.

"Ignore it Riordin," said Mitch. "He's harmless."

"I didn't come here to be made fun of," she mumbled as Warner waved his hand to follow him.

"Please come," he motioned. "Please come."

Warner signalled to Mitch and to Lisa to come inside his cabin. Mitch turned to Lisa and opened his palms as a gesture for her to accept the invitation. She walked sullenly with Mitch to the tin shack.

"I want to show you something. Please come."

Inside, the shack was crammed full of odds and ends. In addition, there was the overwhelming smell of unwashed clothes and mouldy food. Warner scrounged around to find two Boxes and turned them on their side as stools. He motioned for Mitch and Lisa to have a seat on two upturned crates.

"Dis rain. Very bad. I have to get pump working all night or I drown, no?"

Mitch grinned. "So how are you going old timer? Still looking for Dead Man's Reef."

Warner closed the shack door. He waved his hands and moved back toward Mitch.

"Can dis vooman be trusted?"

Mitch nodded affirmatively.

"I think I am close no," said Warner. "I am very close. I tell you because you are my friend Mitch. I tell, you tell no one else da?"

"So you've found it?" asked Mitch.

Warner frowned. He stood up and shuffled to a rickety bench near the wall. He started throwing off mouldy clothes and tools onto the floor. He stopped, turned around holding a bottle of whisky and three rusty cups. He moved back to Mitch and pours two whiskeys. He then signalled to Lisa if she would like one. She shook her head negatively. Mitch sipped at his cup of whisky.

"Jeez, Warner," spluttered Mitch. "You'd kill someone with this one day."

"I tell you because you are my friend," grinned Warner. "I am close. Very close."

Warner shuffled around to the back of the cabin and returned holding an old burlap sack. He lumped it on the table in front of Lisa and Mitch, emptying the contents. It was shavings of different sized quartz.

"I pulled dis out in past few days," said Warner. "I pulled this out at end of no 2 shaft."

"So what are you saying?" asked Mitch.

"I am close," replied Warner. "Tell no one."

Mitch smiled and nodded, looking at his watch and then over at Lisa. He got up from the crate and headed to the door, followed by Lisa.

"I'll come up and see you next week OK?" said Mitch to Warner, before stepping out into the rain and the mud.

Warner turned to Lisa and smiled again, following them both back to the police truck.

"A police vooman. A nice police vooman," repeated Warner. "But Sick. She needs to rest."

Mitch started the truck, turned it around and headed back toward town.

"So what's the story with him?" asked Lisa, as she coughed.

"Albert's been chasing a myth for thirty years. Believing that the miners missed one last great shaft of gold and quartz- dead man's reef."

"Did they?"

"No," said Mitch, shaking his head. "Warner is not even his real name. It's Warnburg, but everyone call's him Warner. All the gold was on the other side of town. Warner's been digging in the wrong place..."

The two way radio in the truck squawked into action as Lisa coughed again.

"Warratama station?, this is Geraldton command. Over," the female voice said. "Warratama station?"

Mitch picked up the two way. "Warratama. What's up?"

"Mitch, there's an accident about a hundred miles up the road from your location," replied the voice on the radio. "Two unidentified fatalities. A Ford station wagon, hit a Roo burst into flames. Coroner is on the way. Can you still get out and review?"

"I'm on my way. Out."

Chapter 4

Mitch placed the microphone of the two way radio back in its holster and turned to Lisa.

"I'm dropping you back at the Grand. Get some rest and I will see you in the morning. You don't have to come out."

Lisa shrugged and coughed again. A few moments later, the police truck pulled up outside the Grand Hotel and Lisa stepped out into the rain and then up to the main verandah and entrance. Mitch wound down the window and called out to Lisa.

"Get some rest," he yelled. "See you in the morning. Greta will help you."

Lisa stepped out of the truck and up to the entrance of the hotel, as Mitch then sped away.

****

The torch briefly spotlit the sexist calendar on the fridge, before Lisa focused on the hallway connecting from the kitchen. She opened the door into the main part of the station, keeping the torch light low to the ground.

At the messy desk of Mitch, she then started to lift papers on the desk, before investigating the drawers. "Nothing," she huffed.

Fever

She got up from the desk, careful to leave everything the way it was and retraced her steps back down the hallway to the bedroom.

Inside the bedroom, she checked the side table. Still nothing. Lisa then moved over to a cabinet and slowly opened the door. There, on the inside of the door was plastered newspaper articles dated to 1995 and a car crash by two detectives Graeme Cassidy and Mitchell Rory, when Cassidy was killed and detective Rory badly injured.

"Bingo," she said, before closing the door and exiting the station via the kitchen.

****

Sitting on a bed in a bathrobe, her head covered in a towel, Lisa was scanning the screen of a laptop, next to a bunch of papers and large brown envelope, when the phone next to the bed rang. She picked it up.

"It is Greta, dear. Now remember like I said, rub the Vicks in and then put on your socks straight away. You'll be right as rain."

"Yes thank you again Greta," said Lisa in reply. "Got it. Bye."

Lisa retuned back to looking at her computer when the landline phone rang again.

"Greta, I've got to keep going," snapped Lisa.

"No, Jim Miles Lisa," said the officious sounding male voice.

"Oh, Assistant Commissioner," said Lisa sheepishly, going bright red with embarrassment, before coughing. "Sorry, I thought you were the receptionist."

"Is everything alright Inspector? I have been trying your phone for a day now, with no answer" said Assistant Commissioner Miles.

"Fine sir. Unfortunately it is bad reception here. Plus the rain."

"What in God's name are you doing up there?"

"I am just doing my job sir."

"You could just have easily sent letters. I certainly hope this has nothing to do with anything personal?"

"No sir. Absolutely not."

"And Senior Sergeant Rory?"

"No, not yet," replied Lisa. "It will be on his desk by tomorrow morning."

"OK. Hand him the paperwork first thing. I've seen the weather report and. Get over your cold and get out of there before you're flooded in. I need you back in

Perth before the end of the week. I don't want you being stuck in some small town up there Inspector, OK?"

"Yes sir."

Lisa hung up the phone and looked over at the brown envelope. She felt the edges in her hands and then put it down.

****

On a cordoned off section of unsealed highway, three high beam lights puncture the veil of steady rain, focusing their attention on the now burnt out shell of the Ford station wagon seen earlier. In front of the wreck was standing Mitch in his wet weather gear, next to a forensics officer (Phil) in a white jump suit and camera. Another forensic officer (Susan) was at the back of the wreck, taking measurements.

"We found the Roo, about thirty metres back along the road," said Phil. "A big red."

Mitch and Phil, the forensic officer step closer to the front of the car, where two mostly burned bodies, one of an elderly man and a woman are still in the drivers and front passenger seats, semi upright.

Chapter 4

"Just two fatalities?" asked Mitch, as Phil nodded his head.

Mitch looked at the wreck and then back at Phil, before adjusting his wet weather gear.

"But if it was just a roo, you wouldn't have called me out in this, or got dressed up," he said.

Phil smiled as he looked over at Susan who signalled for them to come to the back of the wreck.

"Sergeant," said Susan the forensics officer, "you better have a look."

Mitch stepped over to the back of the car, where Susan had dropped to all fours on the ground, pointing a flash light underneath the car. Mitch followed suit.

"What am I looking for?" he asked.

"See, there," she said, waving the flash-light at a cavity extrusion in the underlying chassis of the car. "What don't you see, Sergeant?"

"Any kind of hole," he replied, as Mitch picked himself up off the muddy road, followed by Susan, now filthy in her white jump suit.

Mitch let the rain help clear some of the mud off his hands, before he wiped off the rest of the dirt against his wet weather gear.

"So the fuel tank wasn't ruptured," he grinned. "We have ourselves a double homicide."

Phil and Susan nodded in agreement, as Mitch stepped back to survey the whole wreck, while a flat bed tow truck arrived, with its light flashing.

"How long before all this wraps up?"

Phil pointed to the flat bed tow truck. "Once we get it on the flat bed, we're done."

"Can you do me a favour Phil," said Mitch, "when you send the report to Homicide, can you send a copy of the ID's of the two to Warratama?"

"I can't email it," replied Phil, "because they will ping me. But do you still have an old fax machine?"

Mitch smiled.

"Give me a couple of days then Mitch," added Phil.

Chapter 5

Lisa was dressed in casual clothes, sitting on her own at Antonios Tandoori Italian Restaurant opposite the hotel. One of just three other customers in a restaurant that seated fifty. She was too preoccupied with making shapes with some salt on the table to notice Karl before he walked up to the table.

"Having fun?" he smiled.

Lisa looked up at Karl and blushed.

"Oh, no," she replied hesitantly. "I am just in another world, waiting for the waitress."

"I am an expert at taking hostages and negotiations," he grinned. "Want me to grab her?"

Lisa laughed and smiled nervously as Karl pointed to a chair on the other side of the table. Lisa nodded.

"Sure," she said.

The waitress (Shannon) finally appeared and headed over to the table, immediately engaging with Karl while ignoring Lisa.

"Hello, I'm Shannon. What can I get you?" she beamed. "Me?"

Karl picked up the menu at the centre of the table, pretending not to recognise the blatant flirt.

"Do you have a wine list? Or champagne maybe?"

"I am very sorry," replied Shannon, "but we only have port wine. But we have beer."

"Port?" said Karl sarcastically. "What kind of Italian restaurant is this?"

Antonio popped his head out from the Kitchen like a meerkat. He hurried over to Karl and Lisa.

"Sir, my mother was Italian. My father was Hindu," he said to Karl indigently. "It is due to our regular clientele. I am sorry our clientele only require hard liquor. "

"It's fine," said Lisa. "I'll have a beer."

Karl looked at Lisa and then to Antonio.

"Two beers then," signalled Karl to Shannon the waitress.

Shannon the waitress shuffled off with Antonio.

"A strange place," grinned Karl at Lisa. "The guy fixing my car is Chinese but sounds more Aussie than Crocodile Dundee."

"His family probably were Chinese that came here generations ago for mining," smiled Lisa in reply.

A brief awkward silence.

"So which part of America are you from originally?" she asked.

"I'm not."

Fever

"Oh, but your accent," she said, a little embarrassed. "Sorry Canadian then?"

"Podolia. Western Ukraine. Actually, old Poland. My parents sent me to American school when I was six and then onto college. So the accent stuck."

Karl could see that Lisa still remained pre-occupied by her perceived conversational error.

"So now it is my turn," he said gently. "Why would such a beautiful woman who lived for a time in Arizona or New Mexico want to escape to this part of the world?"

"How did you know I lived in New Mexico?" she said, perplexed and a little shocked.

"Don't worry," he smiled. "People tell you everything you need to know, if you listen carefully and watch them. For example, virtually every large country has different dialects - even if they are subtle. In your case, it sounds like one of your parents was American, but the other, let me guess was probably Australian?"

"My father," said Lisa, choking up. "He was Australian."

"I am sorry, I didn't mean to upset you."

Lisa waved her hand, trying desperately to compose herself. "No, it is fine. It happened a long time ago," she said. "It is just a little raw at the moment, because I have been thinking about him."

"Is it why you have come all the way from civilisation to this place?"

"In a way, yes. He was a police detective, but died when I was still very young."

"I am truly sorry," smiled Karl. "Enough of the questions. My name is Karl. Karl Ratzner."

Karl extended his hand to Lisa.

"Lisa Riordin."

"A pleasure to meet you Lisa."

She wiped her eyes and smiled. "How do you know all these things seriously? and what brings you to this place?"

At that moment Shannon the waitress interrupted them, handing over the two beers.

"You're cheating," said Karl, ignoring Shannon the waitress. "It is still my turn."

"Sorry."

"Let us then imagine for a moment, we are meeting for the first time by chance upon a boulevard of Paris, or an ancient street of Rome. Here then is to life."

****

Fever

Warner chipped away in his mine. A slow methodical waltz, like an old painter. A few taps then a break, shifting some tools and repositioning, then a few more taps.

Warner focused his attention at a hole he had chiselled out of the wall of quartz. A few more taps, then again, only this time there was a loud crack and the wall of quartz and rock fractures in front of him causing dust and dirt to fill the mine. Warner picked himself up as his face was now illuminated not only by his lights, but a gold glow as he stares at an extraordinary sight in front of him.

"My God," he exhaled at the sight in front of his eyes.

****

Empty beer glasses, plates of pasta and Indian food and a wine bottle crowded the table. Lisa and Karl remained entranced by each others company in a now bustling restaurant.

"So tell me more about your geology work?" she asked him.

"What is there to tell? A rock is a rock," said Karl shrugging his shoulders.

Lisa laughed.

"You're being modest," she replied. "To get a job like the one you were saying in Brunei is really something."

"No, its nothing really. They needed someone to help them fix things and I am a fixit man."

Lisa looked over at Karls hands. He spotted her looking for the signs of any ring mark.

"No, not married," replied Karl, his face suddenly tightening. "Not any more. I was married once. No children. My wife Stephanie died in an accident three years ago."

Awkward silence as Lisa put her hand up to her face. She looked around and then back at Karl who had his head down, before she spotted Mayor Dick entering the restaurant.

"I, I am so sorry," she said hesitantly as Karl looked up at her.

"There is nothing to be sorry about," replied Karl softly. "How could you know? We have only just met."

"Constable Riordin!" interrupted the Mayor, now standing over the table of Lisa and Karl. "Or may I call you Lisa?"

Lisa looked up at the Mayor.

"Lisa is fine," she said.

"A Police Officer?" said Karl with a look of surprise. "You didn't share with me that minor detail?"

Lisa blushed in embarrassment, before looking over at Mayor Dick.

"Mayor this is Karl Ratzner. He's a geologist. Karl, this the Mayor of Warratama."

Karl extended his hand and greeted the Mayor.

"Nice to visit your town Mayor," smiled Karl.

"Ah, an American geologist excellent!" bubbled the Mayor. "I am Mayor Dick Masters. But you can call me Dick. I didn't receive any notice, but are you doing a survey of the goldfields perhaps?"

Karl shook his head.

"Just passing through," added Karl. "My car needs a new windscreen. As soon as it is fixed, I'll be on my way."

"Better hurry. The town gets cut off during the rainy season and they say it might happen tomorrow. You may end up touring the goldfields after all."

Outside the restaurant there was an eruption of shouting, laughter and cheers, as Lisa looked past the Mayor to try and catch a glimpse of what was happening.

Shannon the waitress came rushing in from outside brimming with excitement.

Chapter 5

"He did it," she screamed. "He's found it."

Shannon the waitress ran past Karl and Lisa and into the kitchen. Karl and Lisa looked at each other perplexed. She then bounded out of the kitchen, still babbling as she rushed past.

"He's found it," yelled Shannon. "We're rich."

"Who? what's been found?" asked Lisa.

"That darling old man Warner," smiled Shannon to Lisa. "He's found Dead Man's Reef."

Lisa and Karl looked at each other before they ignored the Mayor and got up from their table. They stepped across toward the commotion at the hotel.

Inside, the Main Bar of the Hotel was rapidly filling with people. At the centre of the room was Warner, looking straighter in posture. Next to him was his familiar sack. On the table next to where he was standing was a huge nugget of gold.

"Yeehaa! Drinks all round," yelled Warner, lifting up his beer. "Da beer is on me!"

Music was playing loudly and people are swarming around Warner like flies at a picnic party. Mayor Dick entered the bar and interrupted.

"Good on you Warner old son," grinned Mayor Dick, slapping Warner on the back. "You've put us back on the map. Drinks are on me!"

Andre the barman gave a loud cough.

"But you're broke," said Andre to Mayor Dick, before the Mayor waved his head.

"Today maybe," replied Mayor Dick, "but by first thing tomorrow, before the roads close, I'm going to have every media and prospector from here to Broken Hill in Warratama."

Lisa squeezed through to try and get to where Warner was standing. Through the tight crowd, Warner spotted Lisa and his face lit up.

"My beautiful police vooman," he smiled. "My beautiful vooman. You bring me luck."

Before Lisa could do anything, Warner put his arms around Lisa and bent her slightly over as he gave her a big hug and a kiss on the cheek. Karl was watching to the side, disapprovingly. Lisa managed to break the embrace.

"What a wonderful thing Warner," said Lisa.

"You can call me Albert, my beautiful vooman," added Warner.

Warner tried to hug her again. Lisa moved out of position. She looked over to Karl who moved forward, blocking the advances of Warner.

"Albert, I would like to introduce Karl," said Lisa pointing to Karl. "He is a geologist."

Chapter 5

Warner ignored Karl and continued to smile at Lisa.

"I just want to talk to you, my beautiful police vooman."

Karl stepped in between and extended his hand to Warner.

"It is a pleasure to meet you Mr Warner," said Karl.

Warner's face immediately tightened as he stared at Karl, before Karl spoke to him in Polish.

"It is good to see a person also from the old country who has found their dream," said Karl as people looked on puzzled.

Warner's eyes widened. He rushed forward and embraced Karl, replying in Polish.

"You are from Poland too?" asked Warner.

"Near the border in a small village called Stubice near the Oder River," replied Karl in English.

"Ahh," said Warner.

Warner patted Karl on the back.

"I am only visiting," added Karl. "If it would not be too much trouble, I would be interested in having a look at the formations around your mine?"

"No, it is mine," snapped Warner.

"He doesn't want to steal your gold Albert," added Lisa. "He just wants to have a look."

Fever

Warner rubbed his chin for a moment and then adjusted his taped glasses. He looked at Lisa and then back at Karl.

"Ok. Ok, but just you and the beautiful police vooman."

Lisa looked at Karl. Karl smiled at Lisa.

****

Warner and Karl pulled back the covers over the ladder down into the mine shaft while Lisa in a raincoat steadied an outside lamp.

"Warner my friend. I am happy to go first to make sure Lisa doesn't fall," said Karl.

"OK, OK," nodded Warner, "but be careful the ladder is slippery from dis damn rain."

Karl nodded and waved to Lisa as he descended the shaft.

"My beautiful police vooman, I vill go next to make doubly sure you are fine."

"I'm fine really," said Lisa.

Warner gave a toothless smile and descended the ladder. Lisa followed suit.

Chapter 5

Karl was waiting at the bottom of the mine shaft with Warner while Lisa finally descended. There was about a foot of water on the floor of the mine.

"Now be careful, said Warner. "Dis damn rain is making the floor of the mine very slippery."

Warner had set up lights at various intervals along the mine until the most recent section.

"I have not put lights from here," he said. "We go by torchlight."

Warner turned on an oil lamp, while Karl and Lisa both switched on their torches. As they walked along, Karl noticed a smaller nugget that Warner had left with some other quartz on a bench next to the side tunnel. He quickly took it and put it in his pocket. He stepped forward to keep up with the other two. They finally get to the end of the tunnel where there was a wall of quartz, partly obscured by a large blanket.

"Now my beautiful lady and gentlemen," said Warner, "let me introduce you to a most beautiful site.."

Warner pulled away the blanket to reveal a solid line of gold at least half a foot thick embedded through the quartz.

"Dead Man's Reef," grinned Warner.

Lisa and Karl's mouths and eyes were wide open.

Fever

"My god," gasped Karl. "Is it real?"

Karl rushed forward and touched the thick vein of gold.

"It is real," said Warner.

"It is beautiful," said Lisa.

"Yes it is," added Karl.

****

Karl and Lisa walked in through the main door to the reception area of the Hotel.

"Thank you Karl," she smiled.

"It is not every night that you have the chance to have dinner then show a girl a wonderful discovery such as that," he said.

"Don't forget the mud and the rain."

Karl laughed.

"Yes, yes," chuckled Karl, "the mud and the rain as well. Well I had a wonderful night as well."

Lisa looked at him.

"Coffee?" he asked hesitating.

"Another time," Lisa replied.

Karl moved closer to kiss her. At the last minute Lisa turned her head so the kiss was on her cheek.

"Good night Karl."

Chapter 5

"Good night. Constable Riordin."

****

Karl was sitting on his bed, making notes on a pad. He reached over to a satellite phone and punched in the number. He waited for the phone to answer. A voice answered.

"Peter?"

Peter was standing on a dock, next to the moored boat.

"Yes, Karl. We're here to pick you up. Where are you? What is happening?"

"A change of plans," replied Karl.

"What do you mean?" asked Peter.

"Gold. Lots of it. Ten times our fishing expedition."

"Where?"

"Warratama," replied Karl. "Get the packages and call me when you get here."

"But Karl, this is the second time you have changed the mission in less than a week."

"Do you doubt what I said? Or are you just questioning my orders?"

"No, no, It is not that. It is just the men."

"Tell them the orders and get here asap," growled Karl. "Oh, and I am emailing you across a list of equipment and lights you will need to pick up on the way."

Karl hung up the phone and looked at the specimen he borrowed from Warner.

Chapter 5

Chapter 6

The next morning, the rain was torrential. Mitch was stuck in the police station front office frantically making calls, while outside, cars and trucks continued to rumble into town. The fly-wire door to the station sprung open and Mitch looked up. It was Lisa, in a dark business suit.

"Very flash," he said dryly, cupping his hand over the phone receiver. "Where's your uniform constable?"

Lisa was stone faced. She handed over a brown envelope to Mitch.

"What's this?" he asked as he ripped open the envelope and started to read its contents. Mitch hung up the phone abruptly. "Dear Sergeant Mitchell, blablabla. What? They're offering me redundancy?" A look of shock crept onto his face. "What's going on?" He narrowed his gaze onto Lisa still standing, without a hint of emotion. "Who are you?"

"Look, sergeant. It's nothing personal," Lisa replied nonplussed.

"Who are you really?" growled Mitch, as the phone started ringing.

"Inspector Riordin. From the restructure taskforce." Lisa allowed herself to take a breath, steadying herself. "The decision has been made to change how we manage the Kimberley area. We now have more mobile units, helicopters, planes."

"When?"

"Last month. I'm sorry," she said, even more unconvincingly.

"Last month? Hold on a second. How? Who?" yelled Mitch as the phone continued to ring. "I mean isn't there any report, any damn right of reply first? I mean.. they, you have already closed down three to four stations in a four hundred mile radius from here. What do you expect is supposed to happen when someone needs the police? Are they to somehow magically fly to Perth?"

"The change over doesn't take effect for another month or so," added Lisa.

"Hold on. You haven't answered my question," replied Mitch. "I don't even know if you are who you say you are, even if you're an Inspector? It could all be bullshit?"

"Call Perth yourself. I was seconded from the public relations branch to work on this project."

Mitch picked up the phone and pressed the phone button. "Warratama Police. Can't speak. Call back," he yelled and pressed the cancellation receiver. "So who is the idiot you report to?" he snapped at her. "Who's the useless stupid prick that dreamt up this stupid idea?"

"Deputy Commissioner Miles," Lisa said defiantly. "It's at the bottom of the letter and you don't have to be so rude and insubordinate Sergeant."

Mitch, pressed the numbers into the phone. But a few moments later he cancelled the call and slammed the phone handset down. He got up from the desk and started pacing around the station.

"Goddam."

He put his hands on his head before kicking one of the chairs across the room.

"Damn useless pricks. I've got hundreds of people spilling into this town in the middle of the rainy season. All with gold in their eyes. We're closing the road this morning which means all these idiots are going to be stuck here creating havoc and I've got some snotty courier from puzzle palace telling me that it doesn't fit into their plan. Great. Just great. So why did you put on the game about being my assistant? Do you like to play with your prey before you kill it?"

Lisa frowned and moved back around the office.

"Look I didn't have to come all the way from Perth to the Kimberley's. I asked to-"

"No, there's more to this, I can feel it," interrupted Mitch, causing Lisa to turn red.

"You're the one with the drinking problem sergeant, not me," she snapped back. "Don't blame your sins on me, just because you can't hold it together."

"Oh really? Is that's what you think after being here five minutes? Well, whoever you are," boomed Mitch, "you'll have to call the execution party off a bit for a while. Right now I've got a whole town and district gone to hell to worry about."

Mitch looked at her with disgust as the phone in the station started to ring again.

"OK, get in your truck," he growled. "You're the last one off this boat, before we close the roads and cast off until the rain ends. Get the hell out of my town."

Lisa looked at him in astonishment. "I am your superior Senior Sergeant."

"Not in this town," Mitch replied defiantly as the phone continued to ring. "In this town I am the Sheriff. Full Stop. Now get out!"

"You really don't give a damn about anyone you hurt do you sergeant," she growled. "I've got a few things to pick up from here first before I leave this shithole of yours."

Fever

Lisa stormed out of the station. Mitch picked up the call.

"Rory it's Crane," the voice said abruptly. "Don't you pick up the phone any more?"

"Sorry sir," replied Mitch.

"I heard your Mayor interviewed over the phone on the news. What's the latest situation?" asked Crane.

Lisa stormed back into the station and picked up her bag. But instead of leaving, she stood defiantly, waiting for Mitch to finish the call.

"In a manner of speaking, it's all gone to shit sir," replied Mitch. "There's probably over six hundred people that have arrived in the past three hours and maybe ten times that up on the roads. No media have rolled up yet. "

"I've got twenty men coming up to you by tomorrow morning."

"That's not going to be enough sir," replied Mitch. "Plus the creek is flooding. In an hour the road will be cut off from both ends of the town."

"I don't have the budget for helicopters Sergeant, so how can I get them in?"

"Don't worry, we'll use the old pontoon at Lazy Creek Bridge to ferry them across," said Mitch.

Chapter 6

Mitch glared at Lisa. "On top of all this shit, I've got some woman here from Miles's restructuring plaything telling me we've got to close down the station."

Lisa crossed her arms and stared at Mitch. "Go to hell," she growled.

"She is standing in front of me," said Mitch. "Do you want me to put you on speaker sir?"

Mitch pressed the speaker button on the phone and hung up the receiver.

"To whom am I speaking?" boomed a loud voice from the speaker.

"Inspector Riordin, special taskforce -"

"Yes, yes, I know all that," said Crane, interrupting Lisa. "You're speaking with Deputy Commissioner Crane. Look Inspector, I've got a damn Head of State visit in Perth all this week. Even if I wanted to give the Sergeant more resources, my hands are tied. Until the forces under Acrob get there, you're staying to support Sergeant Rory. Next Sunday you can have all the men you want. Until then, I've spared you all I can. Meanwhile, Miles's girl stays."

"But Deputy Commissioner I am due back in Perth," protested Lisa.

"I don't care," said Crane. "I'll memo Miles now. I don't give a shit what you do."

Fever

"Mitch, hand cuff her to a desk or a lamp post. It's your call."

The phone goes dead.

"Great," huffed Lisa.

****

A sea of people had descended upon the muddy foothills around the outskirts of Warratama. Cars and trucks were bogged in the mud as people leave them where they stopped. Tents of every colour and size now dot the landscape.

People were fighting and scratching every foot in search of gold. Occasionally someone leapt up and jumped for joy as they found the odd gold piece not found in the previous rush.

Others worked earnestly on digging in search of the remainder of the gold streak found by Warner.

****

In the constant rain, Mitch padlocked a barrier at the far end of the main bridge into town, over the flooding creek. Warning signs hung on the barrier that the bridge was closed for flooding.

Chapter 6

****

At the police station, Lisa was busily answering phone calls.

"I'm sorry Mrs Gratham," said Lisa politely to the lady on the phone, "there's nothing I can do about the miners. Yes I understand the mess they've caused at the back of your property. We have more police coming tomorrow."

She hung up the phone. Almost instantly the phone rang again.

"Warratama police," said Lisa.

"Yes, Lisa Riordin please?" asked the male voice.

"Speaking."

"Lisa. It's Karl."

"Hi Karl," said Lisa hesitantly. "Sorry, I didn't recognise it was you. It has been so hectic."

"Yes, I understand. I was wondering if you would like to have dinner tonight?"

"I can't speak right now, things have gone mad," she replied. "The roads are now closed. But until reinforcements arrive from Perth tomorrow morning, its chaos."

"Yes. I've seen all the cars and trucks arriving all day now. So how will they get in?"

"An old pontoon at the creek. I'm not really sure," replied Lisa. "I was supposed to leave today anyway."

"Well if you don't make it out, maybe later then," said Karl.

"Yes, thank you," said Lisa and hung up the phone, before it rang again.

****

The Grand Bar was packed full of muddy and sweaty people. Arguments, boisterous laughter and yelling erupt sporadically as people continue drinking. At the centre of the throng, a circle has formed around two (Marty and Aaron) men fighting.

"Give me back that fifty," yelled Marty.

"You lost it fair and square," protested Aaron.

Marty produced a knife. "I'm going to get my money, if I have to kill you," he growled.

Mitch pushed his way through the crowd to the two men.

"Put it down," demanded Mitch to Marty.

"It's got nothing to do with you. This bastard stole fifty dollars of mine."

Chapter 6

"It was fair game," said Aaron. "He bet fifty dollars against my cards and lost."

Marty, still holding the knife, tried to manoeuvre around Mitch.

"Hang on. Hang on," said Mitch, "it's fifty bloody dollars."

Mitch looked at Marty with the knife.

"Do you want to go to jail for ten years over fifty lousy dollars? Do you?"

"I'll cut anyone that gets in my way," yelled Marty. "I want my money."

Mitch put his hands up.

"Let's sort this out," he said.

Mitch turned to Aaron. "Give him his money back."

"What?" protested Aaron.

"Give him his money back, or I'll throw YOU in jail," said Mitch sternly. "You've got ten seconds."

"Jesus," moaned Aaron. "He's the guy who's got the knife. Not me."

"Five seconds left," said Mitch.

Mitch pulled out his hand cuffs.

"It's not fair. It's not fair," complained Aaron.

"Times up," said Mitch as he reached forward at Aaron, whipping open his hand cuffs. "Turn around."

Fever

Just as Mitch had secured the first arm to slap on the handcuffs, Aaron reached into his pocket with his free hand and produced a crumpled fifty dollar note, throwing it at Marty.

"Here's your lousy fifty bucks."

Mitch undid the first loop of his hand cuffs and put them away, before moving over to Marty as he lent down to pick up the fifty dollars from the floor.

"I'll have that knife too, thanks," said Mitch.

At first Marty hesitated, before huffing and then handing over the knife. Mitch then swung around and addressed the watching crowd.

"Tomorrow morning, there's fifty police coming up from Perth," he yelled. "If we find anyone fighting, they'll be put in jail. If we find any people drunk, we'll throw them in jail. If any of you folks from out of town so much as think of trouble, you can sleep it off in a crowded cell."

Mitch pushed through the crowd back towards the entrance of the hotel.

****

Lisa and Karl were standing in the hotel hallway outside of Lisa's room.

Chapter 6

"Thank you for the dinner and company," she smiled.

"It is the least I could do, considering the day you have had."

Lisa pulled out her room key and gave Karl a look. He touched her hand, before shaking his head negatively.

"Given everything that is going on, I don't know if it such a good idea."

Lisa frowned at him, before Karl waved his hands.

"No, don't get me wrong. You are absolutely beautiful and I know I am going to regret it in ten minutes, but I want to get to know you more first."

"Great. I have found the only man left in the world with morals," she sighed, as she opened the door.

With that, Karl grabbed her by the hand and kissed her passionately. Karl then pulled back.

"Just remember Lisa Riordin that sometimes there may be more that which meets the eye. Especially with Sergeant Mitch Rory."

"What? That he is a psychopathic pig that keeps newspaper cuttings of the death of my father as some kind of sick trophy?"

Karl laughed nervously. "Everyone has secrets Lisa. Everyone has reasons. He could have kept those memories because he doesn't want to forget what he did. You don't know that yet."

Lisa reached over and kissed Karl again.

"Wow a geologist, a philosopher and a gentleman. Good night Karl Ratzner," she smiled.

"Goodnight Inspector Riordin," smiled Karl, as Lisa closed her room door.

****

Mitch was sitting back at the police station, slouched over a desk with his shirt half open. An unopened bottle of whisky prominent in view. He was looking over a photo album.

The first photo was of a younger Mitch as a detective. Next to it was a family photo of Mitch with his wife and two kids. Over the page was a photo of Mitch being awarded a medal for bravery with his partner Graeme Cassidy. Next to the photo was a crumpled and faded newspaper article from 1995 about the car crash of the two detectives. Mitch peeled it open. Next to the article was the picture of a crumpled car and the headline *Hero Cop Charged With Drunk Driving. Partner killed in crash.*

Chapter 6

Mitch tightened the top of the bottle of spirits back up and tossed it into a bin next to the desk.

****

Karl, still fully clothed, was lying on his bed when his satellite phone started to ring. He picked it up.

"Yes. Hello," he said.

Peter was in a van speaking on the phone. Behind him in the van were three other men (Marko, Felix and Elias). "We're here," said Peter.

At the pontoon station, there was a second van of exactly the same type positioned immediately behind Peter's van, being driven by another short haired man (Gunther) and three more men (Stepan, Leon and Omer).

Karl hung up the phone and rolled over, closing his eyes.

Chapter 7

A convoy of 4WD police vehicles pulled up at the pontoon station at the edge of the heavily swollen creek. Over the other side of the flooded creek was the ferry barge with three men on it.

A policeman got out of the first truck and waved to the men on the barge on the other side to come across. One of the men turned around. It was Peter.

****

Inside the police station Mitch was manning one phone, Doc was on another with Lisa on yet another phone at the other side of the main office area. Marjory was ferrying between them, with cups of tea and coffee.

"I've got to go Barry," said Mitch impatiently. "I'm still waiting for the reinforcements to arrive."

He looked over at Lisa who was waiving at him.

"Sergeant, an urgent call," she said

"Speak later," said Mitch into the phone, before hanging up. "What?" he asked in a monotone voice.

"There's a local lady on the phone," said Lisa. "She's hysterical. She lives next to the old Gold Fields.

She says she found two bodies on her property this morning."

"Where?"

"Dead Man's Creek."

Mitch looked at everyone now watching him in the station. "Riordin, your coming with me," he said, before looking over at Doc. "Doc, you're in charge."

Mitch walked across to a cabinet and unlocked the front. Inside was a row of shot guns. On a shelf underneath were boxes of cartridges. He pulled down one of the shotguns and a box of cartridges and started to load the cartridges into the shotgun. Mitch handed the loaded gun to Doc.

"Anyone comes through the door with bad intent. Show them that."

Doc looked at him with shock. "Mitch, I'm a vet. I don't shoot people."

Mitch shook his head. "I don't want you to shoot people either Doc. We won't be long. But just in case, you know it's loaded. And if the worst happens, then you can always fire a warning shot into the air, OK?"

****

Fever

Karl was sitting down with Peter, Gunther and the six other men, at tables in the main bar of the Grand Hotel.

"Whatever your plans are for this godforsaken town," said Peter, "they better be quick before they find them."

"Relax. Relax. The rain is good," smiled Karl. "Let's hope it continues. There's a trapped workforce of worker bees digging away, midst all this chaos."

"You have seen it? It is real?" asked Peter

Karl smiled.

"At least twelve hundred to sixteen hundred kilos," he replied. "Maybe more."

"Kilos of gold, right?" said Gunther.

"But then again, I am only a geologist," sneered Karl sarcastically.

"That's sixty million US dollars," said Peter.

"Did you bring the equipment and the lights like I asked?" asked Karl.

Peter nodded his head positively, before he frowned. "But it is going to take weeks to get all that gold out. We don't have that kind of time with the police and military."

"Three days, maybe two, twenty four hours a day, using the lights, and compression drills. It can be done," said Karl.

"And the authorities?" asked Peter.

"When communication cuts out, of course they'll fear the worst," smiled Karl. "Disasters happen all the time. But here, they don't send the army, they send State Emergency Services. Always do. They even have a Sea King helicopter operating up this region, so it can easily handle the load. As for the two police here now, let them run around trying to keep order. But no one is to touch them, understand."

"What about the longer haul?" asked Gunther.

Karl smiled. "There is an old WWII airfield that is a ten minute flight away. Stepan can contact his friend up at Port Moresby and charter a Dash-8 Q300. We will be fine."

Everyone nodded as Mayor Dick walked through and spotted Karl and the other men.

"Ah Mr Ratzner," smiled Mayor Dick. "Good you're still here."

Mayor Dick looked at the other men, all with short cropped hair and serious intentions.

"Are these colleagues?" asked the Mayor.

"Friends," said Karl.

"Ah, good, well they sure look like they could handle themselves in a fight," replied Mayor Dick with a fake laugh. "Something we need more of at the moment, given the police don't seem to have anything under control."

"Maybe then, they can be of some help Mayor," said Karl. "Have you thought about security until the proper authorities finally get here?"

Mayor Dick rubbed his chin as Karl stepped over and pats him on the back.

"Lets have a chat," smiled Karl.

****

Just up from the embankment of the flooded creek, was a partly submerged brown Holden Ute, wedged next to a Gum tree.

Mitch moved up and had a look, while Lisa stood behind. Inside, two bodies were in the front seats. Their hands were bound and gags were tied around their mouths. At that moment Mitch's mobile phone rings.

"Mitch, it's Marjory," the voice said.

Chapter 7

"It's definitely another double here Marjory," replied Mitch into the phone. "Tell Doc to drive out to help us move the Johnson brothers. What's up?"

"I just got a call from the mine fields," said Marjory through the phone. "Warner is apparently shooting at anything that moves. There may already be a couple of injuries."

Mitch put his spare hand to his head.

"OK. In this rain, there's not much anyone can do for this as a crime scene. Get Doc up here and I'll head over to the mines. I already have a pretty good suspect for this."

Mitch hung up and looked over at Lisa. "Looks like your boyfriend has been busy."

Lisa looked at him strangely. "Excuse me what did you say?"

Mitch turned around and strode back toward the police truck. Lisa follows.

"Have you ever used your firearm Inspector?"

"In training, sure," replied Lisa as they both get into the truck and Mitch starts it up. "What's going on?"

Mitch spun the truck around and floored it back up the track to the goldfields.

"Warner is shooting at anything that moves," he replied.

"What about what you said earlier? Do you think Karl had something to do with those murders?"

"When it is all said and done," grumbled Mitch, "the simplest and oldest motives are usually the first."

"Maybe you are getting too old for this job sergeant," replied Lisa sarcastically. "Whatever happened to innocence before being guilty?"

"It's not rocket science. It's called instinct. A sense of character. It is why fish swim with fish and sharks swim with sharks."

"Thanks Sergeant for your twenty five dollar psychic reading. Let's just get there and sort out Warner."

****

Mayor Dick, Karl, Peter, Gunther and two other men, with military semi-automatic rifles were standing in the rain outside the back of the Grand Hotel, looking at the town generator and phone tower.

"This is it," smiled Mayor Dick. "The main town generator and phone tower. But the hotel also has its own power generator in case of emergencies."

Chapter 7

"I will make sure my friends here guard this place until the authorities finally arrive."

"Thank you Karl," smiled Mayor Dick. "And thank you for the personal security. This town has become like the wild west under Sergeant Mitch Rory."

Karl nodded in agreement.

"Anything to keep this town safe Mr Mayor."

****

The foothills were a sea of mud as the rain continued relentlessly. People were frantically digging in spite of the rain. The entire scene looked like a trench war battlefield. Above the din of shovels and picks, the intermittent sound of a shotgun echoed over the diggings.

"Get off my land you vultures," yelled Warner.

Gun shots rung out again. "Get off my find," screamed Warner.

Mitch pulled up his truck and got out with Lisa.

"Keep your head down," he said.

Two miners ran up to the truck and confronted Mitch.

"He's gone crazy, the old bastard," said the first miner. "He started shooting about half an hour ago."

"I think he's already shot someone," said the other miner. "There's another guy just down from this guy's shack who's bleeding like a stuck pig."

"Can you move him?" asked Mitch.

"Can't even get near him," replied the second miner. "That old bastard is shooting at anything that moves."

Mitch walked back to the truck and got out a megaphone and his shotgun. He walked up the track and stopped just before a rise, out of site of Warner's shack. He turned on the megaphone and tested it. It squawked into action.

"Warner. Can you hear me? It's Mitch."

"Go away," yelled Warner. "Leave. Dis is my gold."

"We know it's your gold Albert," replied Mitch over the megaphone. "Some of these people are trespassing. We'll move them on. But first Albert, you've got to give me your gun."

"They're stealing my gold," protested Warner.

"Look Albert, I can't do anything until you give me your gun."

"They're trying to take my dream. They're robbers... all of them. Stay back."

Warner let off another shot. Mitch instinctively dived for cover into the mud and cursed.

Chapter 7

Two bloodied and battered police constables (Bracken and Dematous) staggered to the front door of the police station and fell inside.

Marjory, Barry the Mechanic and Antonio were busily manning the phones and fielding people making complaints when the two bloodied police officers fell into the police station. There was a collective shriek as Marjory and Antonio leapt over to help the injured men. In the corner, the fax machine whirred into life.

The first page of the fax spat out with photos of Ken and Dorothy, seen earlier as the original occupants of the Range Rover. The second page was a picture of the Range Rover itself, before suddenly the machine stopped, the phones went dead.

"The powers out," yelled Barry.

Antonio desperately punched Doc's number into his mobile phone.

"I can't get Doc," said Antonio.

Marjory had already stripped off the shirts of both men, investigating their wounds.

"There's no time," said Marjory as she signalled to Antonio. "Get the medical kit from the back. Hurry!"

Fever

Marjory looked down at Constable Bracken.

"Don't worry dear. I'm a nurse," she smiled. "Well, a vet nurse. You'll be alright."

Chapter 7

Chapter 8

Mitch and Lisa were still pinned down by Warner.

"Please Albert. Give up your gun," shouted Mitch. "We will get the people away. But we've got to help the people you've shot."

"I'm not moving," yelled Warner in reply.

Mitch handed his shotgun to Lisa. "Albert, I'm coming over. I'm unarmed."

Mitch started to slowly walk toward Warner's shack. "I'm unarmed Warner."

He kept walking toward the shack door. The gun from the shack still pointed at him. "I just want to talk Albert."

Mitch reached the shack door and the gun withdrew. He opened the shack door and entered.

****

Karl and Peter were studying a map of the goldfields in the empty main bar of Grand Hotel. Apart from Karl's henchman, only Andre the barman was present, looking especially nervous.

As Karl and Peter looked at the map, Mayor Dick burst into the main bar. Marko and Leon moved forward and intercepted him, but Karl immediately signalled for them to let him go.

"You turned off the power and cut off the phone lines," yelled Mayor Dick as he approached Karl.

"We had to," said Karl, calmly. "There was no other choice."

Mayor Dick looked at him strangely. "And you have closed down this bar. What is going on?"

"You said it yourself Mayor. Anarchy. People have been jamming the phone service, sending all kinds of texts causing people to risk their lives to come here with Fever. Gold Fever. They have been getting drunk and violent. Haven't you heard about the unsolved murders?"

Mayor Dick nodded his head. "Sure, sure. Everyone has been talking about the Johnson boys murder."

"You asked me to help, because Sergeant Rory is incapable of maintaining order. Or do you want me to reopen the bar so the town is full of drunk and violent strangers?"

The mayor shook his head negatively. "No, no. But I am concerned how it might look."

"Oh you mean the authorities? Sure, it might just get them up here quicker, don't you think? Or do you want me to turn back on the phone tower so this dangerous chaos continues?"

"No, no. I understand," said the Mayor. "Just let me know first OK?"

Karl smiled. "Of course. You are the boss of this town."

****

Mitch led Warner to the police truck in handcuffs, while Lisa walked behind, holding Warner's shotgun. A large crowd of angry miners assembled around them.

"Hang the bastard," someone yelled from the back of the crowd.

"He killed two people," yelled someone else. "String him up."

Mitch turned around angrily. "There'll be no more shooting," he growled. "Go back to your gold digging. Warner will be judged on what he's done in a proper court, not by a lynching mob."

The groans and angry calls increased as the mob closed in on the police truck. Mitch bundled Warner into the back seat and Lisa got in next to him. Then Mitch jumped into the driver's seat, started the engine and turned the truck around, spinning the wheels in

Chapter 8

the mud. The splashing mud forced the mob to back away, creating a gap. Mitch then floored the truck back down the hill.

****

The whole town was dark, except for the Grand Hotel with all its lights still on. Lisa tried her mobile phone again.

"No good," she said. "Can't get a signal."

Mitch didn't slow down as he drove past the hotel.

"We'll get back to the station first, see if Doc and the crew are OK."

Mitch stopped the police truck outside of the Police Station that was eerily lit from candles and small lights from the inside.

As Mitch entered the door dragging Warner behind him, a shotgun was pressed to the back of his head.

"Shit Doc. Take it easy."

Doc quickly pulled the shotgun back as Mitch surveyed the room. He saw two injured police lying on stretchers in the corner, being tended by Marjory.

"What the hell?"

"Ambush Mitch," said the Doc. "It seems someone knew the reinforcements were coming and didn't want the competition."

Mitch swung around and gave Lisa a filthy stare as he pushed Warner toward the cells in the back of the room.

"Don't give me your evil eyes," she protested as Mitch put Warner in a cell. "Oh, so you think Karl is behind killing cops now as well?"

Mitch closed the door on Warner and swung back toward Doc who handed Mitch the incomplete fax pages and a torch to read them. He looked at the photos of Dorothy and Ken and then the second page of the Range Rover before throwing them at Lisa. Her face suddenly went blank when she realised what she was seeing.

"But it can't be- "

"The Constables survived in air pockets in the vehicles until the shooting stopped," said Doc. "They've lost a lot of blood but should survive if we get help in time. All the phones are out and the power except for the Grand Hotel. Definitely foreigners behind all this. Barry and Antonio have seen them up at the Grand Hotel. It seems they report to this Karl fellow."

"But he's a geologist," said Lisa weakly.

Chapter 8

"That kills people and you gave him everything he needs to know," grumbled Mitch.

There was a growing rumbling outside and Barry peered out the window.

"Mitch, You better have a look outside, quick," said Barry.

Mitch walked to one of the windows and looks outside. There were now dozens of cars and trucks blocking the street, their lights creating temporary street lighting. Mud covered miners, some carrying guns started to approach the station.

Mitch moved toward the shotgun rack in the corner, pulling down a second shotgun and loading it, handing it to Barry. He did the same again and handed it to Antonio. The last shotgun he handed to Lisa, before he grabbed his own shotgun lying next to his desk.

"What are you doing?" asked Lisa.

"Screw them," said Mitch. "They're turning my town into Dodge City."

"Mitchell. Give us Warner," yelled a voice from outside.

"Yeah. Give him up and we'll deal with him," said another voice from the mob outside.

Mitch walked to the door.

"Mitch don't. It's suicide," said Lisa.

Mitch turned to the others inside the station.

"If I go down, start shooting. Not before. It might be your only chance."

He swung open the door and walked out. Outside the Police Station a crowd of angry miners had formed. Mitch walked a few steps away from the station and toward the centre of the crowd. At the centre was Mayor Dick and with Karl off to the side, carrying a high powered assault rifle.

"There will be no more killing today," said Mitch. "Warner will get a fair trial and if he's guilty he'll be sentenced."

"We want Warner," yelled one of the mob.

Mayor Dick raised his hands to Mitch.

"Sergeant. All we want is justice. As Mayor, I am the highest authority over the town. Hand over Warner and I promise you he will get a fair trial."

"What about your new offsider?" said Mitch. "Did the police he killed get a fair trial?"

Peter, Gunther and other men of Karl move forward from the crowd, all carrying heavy assault rifles as Karl also moved forward next to Mayor Dick.

"Now Sergeant," smiled Karl. "No one wants to tell you how to do your job. If you have accusations I am sure there will be the right time for making them. But right now, what this town needs is order and you are not bringing it."

"You are not the law," said Mitch. "You're the problem."

Peter and the other men now start to point their guns directly at Mitch as the windows of the police station inch open and shot guns start to appear. Instead of backing off, Mitch moved forward toward Karl.

"Karl Ratzner, you are under arrest on suspicion of the murders of the Johnson brothers and Dorothy and Ken Mayberry."

Karl looked over at Peter and shook his head negatively. The henchmen lowered their weapons as Mitch moved over and handcuffed Karl.

"Sergeant Rory," said the Mayor, "I order you to stop-"

"It's OK Mayor," smiled Karl. "Let Sergeant Rory have his moment."

"Now the rest of you go home or to your tents," yelled Mitch as he turned Karl around to face the police station. "It's over."

"For now," growled Peter.

Fever

Midst hissing and catcalling, Mitch dragged Karl back into the station as the miners and the henchmen start to disperse.

Once inside, Doc shook his head at Mitch.

"What do you think you were doing?" said Doc.

Mitch ignored him as he pushed Karl past towards the cells. Karl looked over at Lisa as he was pushed past and smiled.

"Now they're really going to be pissed and storm this place," huffed Doc.

"Not while their beloved leader is here," replied Mitch.

Mitch finished closing the cell door as he stared back at Lisa, still looking incredulously at Karl, sitting peacefully on a cell bed, watching the show.

Constable Dematous got up onto his feet and shuffled over to Karl in the cell. In an instant he has raised a shotgun towards him.

"You filthy pig. It's time to pay."

Mitch rushed over and pulled the gun away just in time, causing Constable Dematous to stumble and fall back.

"There'll be no summary justice on my watch," yelled Mitch. "He stays here until help arrives."

Chapter 8

Marjory came over and took Constable Dematous back to lie down on a stretcher.

"Bravo. Sergeant," smiled Karl. "Very noble of you. Thank you."

"I didn't do it for you," growled Mitch. "If I had my way. You'd be floating down the creek and out to sea. But its the law."

"Indeed it is," replied Karl. "Innocent as they say, until proven guilty."

"How could you?" said Lisa to Karl. "I trusted you?"

"What is with the surprise?"

"You lied. You lied to me," she said.

"Dear beautiful Lisa, I did not Lie. I graduated as a geologist and I have worked and travelled to the places we discussed."

"But you killed those poor people," she added.

"No Lisa, it is you who is not telling the truth. Do you not carry a loaded gun?"

"Sure, but - "

"And are you empowered to use it," said Karl, interrupting her, "to use deadly force?"

"Yes, but this is - "

"So now you're telling me you have the right to shoot people who may not be attacking you," said Karl, interrupting Lisa again. "But I am not allowed to defend myself?"

"No, that's not what I am saying - "

"I'm sorry Lisa," interrupted Mitch. "Give it a rest. I can now see you were seduced by a snake. Let him rot for a bit."

Mitch pulled Lisa away. "Don't waste your breath."

Chapter 8

Chapter 9

The mines were now lit up by large halogen lights, connected to generators, lighting up the dreary diggings like a hellish third world archaeological site.

Gunther and his team were standing on the tops of different hills along with new recruits from the ranks of the miners. All holding semi-automatic weapons. Below them, dozens of miners continued to work, blackened by the mud. As one slipped or cursed, Karl's men push them back to work.

Slowly a long line of miners, wind up a hill carrying lumps of quartz and gold to a waiting truck, guarded by some of Karl's men. The guards stare intently as the miners load their specs and shavings of gold into the truck tray and return blankly down the hill. A middle aged woman, covered in mud stared for too long into the truck after depositing some gold.

"Get back to work!" yelled one of the guards.

She was pushed forcefully away by one of guards down the hill. She tumbled down into the never ending mud.

One of the younger miner's bringing up gold and quartz looked frantically at Gunther standing next to the truck. As Gunther looked away, the young man made a run for it down the road, ducking and weaving between other miners towards the town. Gunther turned around to see the figure running away.

"Halt," yelled Gunther.

Yet the young miner keeps running. Gunther raised his gun and took aim. People scatter out of the way from the road. He fired twice. The man fell face down onto the road, dead.

****

The Lounge bar of the Grand Hotel had been completely re-arranged. A large decorative chair, elevated on a small platform from the front of the hotel has been moved in and placed against the far wall. The rest of the tables have been pushed back. Peter was sitting in the decorative chair. A group of ten miners were standing in a semi circle in front of the chair with two of Karl's henchmen on either side.

"So you men want to join our merry band?" smiled Peter.

The miners nod.

"You've all shown past history in military service and how to handle a gun," continued Peter. "Very well, the rules for the town are very simple. If someone steals, they are shot. If there is an argument, the people are to be brought before me for judgement."

Mayor Dick pushed through the band of miners to Peter. "Is is true you are now killing miners who don't work hard enough?" he asked.

"Excuse me for a moment," said Peter to the new band of recruits.

"It was you who made the deal Mayor," smiled Peter. "Ten million dollars in gold."

"Well now I'm breaking it," said Mayor Dick. "I want no part of this."

"A man without his word is nothing. If that is your final wish."

"Hold on," said the Mayor as he watched Peter reach down to his side. "I just want to be clear -"

Before the Mayor could finish his sentence, Peter whipped out a pistol and shot Mayor Dick in front of the other henchman. The Mayor fell to the ground dead.

"And there is a perfect example of a justice done," grinned Peter. "So any questions?"

The new miners shook their heads unanimously without speaking.

"Fine, then off to work."

Chapter 9

The miners shuffled out and the henchman Felix moved over to Peter and leant against the decorative chair.

"With these fellows and the twenty-two others that we have signed up, we can have all of the key points covered, including the Police Station," said Felix.

"Good," replied Peter. "How long to strip out the rest of the gold of Dead Man's Reef?"

"If we use explosives, and push the miners, then maybe three to four days."

"Do it in two," said Peter. "Even if you have to shoot a few more in the process."

"But our men will be stretched too thin between melting the gold into bars, the police station and the mines," complained Felix. "When will you give the order to sort out the Police Station, cause -"

Peter put up his right hand as a gesture to stop Felix in mid sentence.

"There will be no storming of the police station. Karl will let us know when he is ready."

"The Lisa girl," grumbled Elias, standing next to Felix.

Peter gave Elias a menacing stare. "Careful soldier. An army survives only as long as its commands are obeyed without question."

Fever

Both Elias and Felix saluted as the body of the dead Mayor was dragged away. Two women started washing up the mess on the floor, while Peter stared out the window at the continuing rain.

****

Inside the Police Station was eerily silent. The two injured policemen were sleeping, along with Warner, Marjory, Lisa and Antonio. Barry struggled to keeps his eyes open keeping watch through one window and Doc was almost asleep looking through another. Only Mitch and Karl were awake. Mitch walked over and handed Karl a glass of water.

"Why do you cling to such a redundant romanticism of law?" asked Karl. "You could have killed me and been over with all of this."

"And yet, I am not the one in love."

"True," said Karl. "Funny how both of us are prisoners of our own conscience."

"You don't have one," snapped Mitch. "Lets get it straight, I don't like you or what your people have done to this town."

"And yet you would risk your life defending someone you hate. Odd."

Chapter 9

"It's over," grinned Mitch. "She knows what you are."

"It's never really over is it Sergeant? Not even for a man who runs to the end of the earth to hide from his demons. No, she knows exactly who *you* are former detective Rory."

Mitch looked shocked by the revelation.

"Oh yes, sergeant Lisa knows all about the drunk man who killed her daddy."

"Shut the hell up!" yelled Mitch, causing Lisa and the others to wake up. Karl observed Lisa was now awake and waited a bit longer.

"You mean, Inspector Riordin hasn't told you her real birth name was Cassidy sergeant?" grinned Karl. "And that the American widow of detective Graeme Cassidy changed her name back to Riordin?"

"Why are you doing this?" screamed Lisa as she leapt over toward the cells, causing Mitch to stand up and stop her from getting closer.

"Don't get angry with me Lisa. You're the one who made your own field trip to finally confront the killer of your dad," said Karl. "You're the one that wanted to exact revenge against Mitch here for what he did. Be honest!"

Mitch looked at Lisa with a look of confusion and sadness.

"It is true," said Lisa. "My dad was Detective Graeme Cassidy. And I did initially come here to confront you. And I saw the newspaper articles you kept out the back in the bedroom. But in the past few days, seeing you, what you do, I have also changed my mind."

Karl started to laugh.

"Now you are really lying Lisa," chuckled Karl. "This is the man, you called a psychopath, holding newspaper articles like some trophy."

"Is that what you think?" asked Mitch. "You crept around and that is why you thought I kept those articles. But the truth is that I have looked at them with regret every day for half of my life?"

"No... well... I didn't understand," stuttered Lisa.

Mitch shook his head. "Graeme, your father was my best mate. I didn't crash the car because I was drunk. I crashed the car because your father was blind drunk. I took the wrap, so your mum didn't lose the pension. There is not a day that I do not think of your father and so I kept those articles as a matter of respect and a reminder."

Chapter 9

Karl bellowed laughter in response was so loud, it woke Warner in the next cell.

"Oh please, spare me the drama," he said, as Lisa looked at Mitch, and both Mitch and Lisa turned around and left him. Karl then turned back to see Warner was awake.

"Why did you do this to me?" said Warner weakly in Polish.

Karl looked at him strangely.

"Why did you destroy me?" added Warner.

"I did not cause you to shoot those miners or be arrested old man," replied Karl softly. "Nor did I disrespect your dream."

"But you and others have taken my gold," protested Warner, coughing in the process.

"Your vision wasn't the gold, it was the glory," said Karl. "Be honest. You wanted to prove everyone else wrong by finding Dead Man's Reef. Well that is exactly what you did and no one can take that from you."

Warner rolled over, with his back to Karl.

Chapter 10

Morning in Warratama as the sun rose over sparsely clouded skies. The sounds of birds and life resuming as the rains had finally stopped.

Mitch awoke from a half sleep as rays of light started to pour into the station. He nervously searched for his shotgun. It was just next to him. He looked around as Doc handed him a coffee.

"Tastes terrible," smiled Doc. "Almost as bad as Antonios Italian. But it wakes you up."

Mitch took a few sips and looked over at the injured police officers.

"The two officers are doing better," added Doc.

"You're the best vet I Know," grinned Mitch.

Mitch looked over at the cells as Karl watched him. Warner was rolled over and not moving in his cell.

"Warner do you want a coffee?" yelled Mitch, to no reaction. Mitch walked over to the cell, eyeballing Karl.

"Don't look at me," shrugged Karl.

"Hey Warner," said Mitch, opening the cell. As he reached him, he could see the face and arms of Warner were white. Mitch looked over at Doc who stepped over and walked into the cell.

"He's dead Mitch. What will we do -"

Fever

Mitch put his hand up and cut off Doc mid sentence as he heard the faint thud of rotor blades below the squawking of the birds and town coming to life.

"They're here," said Mitch.

****

Peter was inside a warehouse next to the Grand Hotel when his ears pricked up. He also heard the sound of rotor blades in the distance. He dropped the gold bars being loaded into boxes and waved at Gunther.

"Outside," yelled Peter. "Quick. Get Stepan and Leon into the police uniforms."

Gunther nodded and ran out of the door of the warehouse.

Peter moved outside and looked up as a State Emergency Services Sea King helicopter swept overhead and then did another circle of the town. He turned the knob on his secure radio set.

****

The State Emergency Services helicopter landed on a grass patch just down from the Grand Hotel. Out of range of the police station, but the only bit of ground not covered in mud. Waiting were Gunther, Stepan and Leon wearing police uniforms. They moved forward to greet the people from the helicopter. One of the emergency personnel stepped off the helicopter.

"Welcome. We thought you'd never get here," smiled Gunther in his police uniform.

"What's happened to the radio and phones? We've been trying to get through?"

"Out. The rain," smiled Stepan, "It's been hell. Two thousand people wildly digging."

"What about food and supplies?"

"Desperate," said Gunther. "We desperately need supplies dropped."

"We're onto it," replied the emergency services officer. "How's Commander Acrob?"

"Commander?" questioned Gunther.

"The reinforcemcnts?"

"Busy," smiled Gunther. "Trying to keep a lid on this place. He's sorry he couldn't make it. He's over at the main hotel."

Just then in the background near the police station, shotguns ring out.

"What the hell was that?"

More gun shots.

"It's OK," smiled Gunther. "Just miners after a find."

The officer from the helicopter looked anxious. He started to walk back toward the helicopter waving at the pilot standing outside. But before he could get much further, guns were pointed at him and the rest of the helicopter crew.

****

Inside the Police Station, Karl looked at Lisa.

"Now that it looks like the cavalry has arrived," said Karl, "I won't have much time to say again, I am sorry you feel the way you do now about me."

"I trusted you," said Lisa. "But like all men it seems, your word is nothing."

"On the contrary. I meant every word I said," replied Karl. "Lisa I would never do anything to harm you or Mitch. I promise."

"You have a strange way of showing it."

"Why do you think I let Mitch take me in the first place?" asked Karl.

Lisa stopped speaking as Mitch put his hands to his lips for everyone in the police station to be quiet. There was the sound of people once again outside of the police station.

"Mitch. We want to talk," a voice yelled.

Mitch inched up to the window and looked outside.

Outside the Police Station and down the main road of Warratama was standing Peter. To the side of him was Gunther, holding a handcuffed and gagged emergency services officer. Further back were the other six henchmen all standing with semi-automatic weapons.

"Come out Mitch. No shooting. I promise."

Mitch stepped outside the Police Station carrying his shot gun and steps slowly towards Peter.

"We have the helicopter Mitch. We've got the crew as hostages as well. Release Karl and we will let the hostages and you all go free."

"I don't do deals with criminals," yelled Mitch. "Put down your weapons. You are all under arrest."

Peter laughed as the henchmen move in closer around the outside of the Police Station.

"Yes, yes, we all saw the John Wayne show earlier. Very impressive. Look, we don't have the time. See that hostage over there. We've got a whole town full of them. One last time, release Karl or we'll start executing them, one by one on your watch.

Chapter 10

Mitch advanced closer to Peter and raised his gun. "Drop your weapon. You are under arrest."

Peter raised his gun and shot at Mitch, who dropped to the ground. At the same instant, the other henchmen strike at the Police Station. Felix was the first who entered and Lisa fired at him, hitting him squarely in the chest. But before she had time to aim again, Marko entered and fired at Lisa, hitting her in her thigh and she collapsed.

The rest of the henchmen entered the Police Station as Peter picked up the shotgun of Mitch and followed in behind. He moved over to Karl in his cell and smiled.

"I ordered no shooting," yelled Karl.

"Always the romantic," replied Peter. "You were wrong about the gold."

Karl looked at him strangely as Peter raised the shotgun toward Karl.

"More like one hundred million. A reasonable pay after wasting half my life following you around the world."

"What are you doing?"

"Giving the authorities their bad guy."

"So that's it. You are just going to double cross me?"

Before Peter could fire, Lisa fired again and hit Peter in the back, causing him to collapse.

"Don't touch her," yelled Karl as Gunther and Leon came over and unlocked the Cell.

Karl walked over to Peter who was barely alive, a look of horror on his face.

"You are such a disappointment."

Karl fired at Peter at close range and finished him off.

"If they're disarmed," said Karl to Gunther, "let them go."

Karl walked to the door and outside.

Lisa was hovering over Mitch, who was still alive, but bleeding from the right shoulder. Doc rushed past Karl with a bag to attend Mitch. Karl moved over as Lisa swung around and glared at him.

"I gave my word and I am sorry," said Karl. "But you need to get help with that wound."

The Doc looked first at Mitch and then at Lisa. The Doc then started to tie a tourniquet around the leg of Lisa.

"It will slow the bleeding, but we need to get the bullet out," he said.

"Is she OK Doc? asked Karl.

The Doc gave Karl a menacing stare.

"What do you think?" he growled. "Your men just shot her in the leg. I need three to four hours to get the bullet out. If it doesn't come out then she will either die of infection or blood loss or both."

"I don't have three hours at the moment. What about Mitch?"

"He'll live," replied the Doc. "But its Lisa I am worried about."

Karl looked over at Lisa.

"The Doc will take care of Mitch. But you and I have to go now."

"I am not going anywhere."

Karl motioned to Elias and Leon to take Lisa away.

"Don't touch me," she screamed.

"Be careful and make sure that tourniquet is secure," said Karl.

Elias and Leon nodded and took her away.

"You promised. You bastard."

Karl, swung around and looked at Lisa being carried by the henchmen.

"Don't get all princess on me now."

The henchmen dragged Lisa away.

****

Fever

Slowly, the State Emergency Services Sea King
helicopter gained altitude and flew away.

Chapter 10

Chapter 11

A convoy of State Emergency Services vehicles rumbled into Warratama and stopped at the scene out the front of the Police Station. Soon after, a military black hawk helicopter landed opposite the police station.

Out of the helicopter stepped an officious looking State Emergency official (Commander John Harney), who walked over to the crowd.

"Whose in charge?" yelled Commander John Harney as he pushed through the crowd outside the Police Station.

There, at the centre, was Mitch, with his arm in a sling, being helped by the Doc.

"I am," said Mitch.

****

Inside the police station, emergency personnel were running around with pieces of paper and communication equipment. Mitch stepped over to Commander Harney who was on a satellite phone.

"Commander, is there any news on the police officer Lisa Riordin and the helicopter they hijacked?"

Fever

The Commander put his hand up. "One sec," he said into the phone, cupping it with his hand. "The helicopter was retrieved at Broome. The local police are tracking down Karl Ratzner and his hostage."

Mitch shook his head. "It is too easy. There is no way this fellow flew straight to Broome."

The Commander shrugged his shoulders. "Excuse me, but I am trying to coordinate relief efforts," he said.

The Commander resumed his phone call as Mitch stood there for a few moments, shaking his head. "This is hopeless," he grumbled.

An emergency worker came running into the police station, flapping his arms at the Commander. "We found the police bodies," he yelled. "We found them!"

Commander Harney huffed and put his satellite phone down.

"Calm down and be clear," growled the Commander.

"We have located the bodies of at least ten police officers near the old pontoon station," he said. "But the pontoon itself is missing."

"Probably collected in the flood," said the Commander.

"No," said the worker, shaking his head negatively. "The ropes were deliberately cut. It is gone."

"There you go!" yelled Mitch. "Like I was trying to say, Ratzner and Lisa are not in Broome."

"OK, sergeant, so where do you think they are exactly?" asked the Commander sarcastically.

****

Three trucks were atop the old bridge pontoon, now powered by out board engines, down the swollen creek.

"They will find you," said Lisa, still wincing in pain.

"Eventually. But not today," replied Karl. "Don't worry. When we get to where we are going soon, Gunther is a trained field medic and will get that bullet out of your leg. You'll live."

"And what about me. Do you plan to kill me?" said Lisa half conscious, her speech slurred. "Or do you plan to lock me up as some kind of slave?"

Karl laughed.

"No. No. When we get to where we are going, you will be free to leave. I just want some quality time to show you I am not a monster."

"I don't think there is enough time in both our lifetimes for tha-."

Chapter 11

Lisa passed out. Gunther approached Karl.

"We need to get that bullet out now and stop the bleeding or she won't make it," said Gunther.

"Here? Now on this pontoon?"

"I've done operations in worse places."

Karl shook his head. "Whatever you do. Make sure she is OK."

****

Mitch and the Commander were looking at a map on his desk.

"If he is carrying the kind of weight I think he is," said Mitch, "then either by truck, which means you would have spotted him on the roads or by boat are logical."

Mitch looked at the map and pointed to a spot.

"If I was a betting man during a big wet. The best landing strip for a cargo plane to carry the gold is the old World War II base at Warrens Farm airfield here."

The Commander looked up at his team.

"Right, alert the special operations Police Command to get up here," said Commander Harney.

"But that will take a day," grumbled Mitch.

"Sergeant, we are emergency services, not the army or police," huffed the Commander.

Mitch pointed to the helicopter outside. "But you have an army helicopter here," said Mitch, clearly frustrated.

"We need that for lifting supplies Sergeant," replied the Commander.

"But they will be long gone, if we keep waiting here."

The Commander shook his head negatively. "I am sorry sergeant, there is nothing I can do," he said.

Mitch stormed out of the police station. He looked down the main street and then across at the helicopter. He nodded to the flight technician (Matt) and pilot (Anna) who were standing in front.

"You heard about what happened here?" he asked them.

"Yes," said the pilot Anna. "Mercenaries, gun fights and all those poor police."

"You know those bad guys are at Warrens Airfield only fifteen minutes away by helicopter," said Mitch. "And thanks to that numb-nut commander in my station, they'll be out of the country by the time your superiors get word."

Chapter 11

Both Matt and Anna shook their heads. As they did, the other pilot (Ewen) stepped outside of the helicopter to hear the conversation.

"It sucks. We'd be up and out of here in a minute if we could," said Ewen. "But we're stuck here until that idiot gives us orders."

"What if there was another way?" asked Mitch.

The soldiers look at him strangely.

"It will be the end of my career and I will probably go to prison, but what if I hijacked the helicopter?"

The three of them all laughed at him, looking at his arm in a sling. Mitch pulled his arm out of the sling and unbuttoned his side revolver. "No I am serious," he said.

****

The pontoon was moving along toward a jetty on the river. Omer and Stepan were already standing on the jetty as the pontoon was brought alongside.

Karl looked down at Lisa, who was asleep on her stretcher, her leg bound with a proper dressing. Some of the men start to unload the boxes until Karl signalled them to look at Lisa.

Fever

Get her across safely, then worry about the boxes, he said.

At that moment, Lisa slowly half opened her eyes.

"Where are we?" she asked, still slurring her words.

"Don't worry. I took care of that bullet in your leg. You are going to be fine."

Lisa frowned and closed her eyes.

"Lisa. Don't look so sad, said Karl. Now you can have anything you want."

"I just want my freedom. Will you give me that?" she asked, still with her eyes closed.

Karl laughed as Marko and Elias gently picked her up and carried her off the pontoon.

"Lisa. In good time. But first, we must take a little flight up the coast to Indonesia. Maybe we can continue where we left off at the Grand Hotel?"

"Ncvcr," she said, before passing back to sleep.

Karl laughed again.

****

In the helicopter, Ewen signalled to Mitch.

"We will be at the airfield in ten minutes," he said. "The commander has already radioed in to our base demanding to know what we are doing. We are keeping radio silent to buy you some time. But pretty soon, they will be checking on us and at that point there will be nothing we can do then."

Mitch nodded. "Just get me down there," he said. "I will get Lisa."

He looked over at the technician Matt. "Do you have anything stronger than a 9mm?"

Matt smiled and unlocked a secure cabinet at the back of the helicopter. In it were a set of semi-automatic weapons and ammunition. Below the weapons was a set of grenades.

"Perfect," smiled Mitch.

Chapter 12

At the Warrens Farm airfield, a Dash-8 was parked out the front of an old aircraft hangar. Karl's henchmen were loading boxes of gold into the back of the plane, while the pilot checked the left engine. Lisa was still sleeping on the stretcher inside the hangar, while Karl and Gunther check a map.

"We are running out of time. What's the pilot doing?" snapped Karl.

Gunther shrugged his shoulders.

"Well go and find out," growled Karl.

Gunther nodded to Karl and walked over to the pilot.

"What's up?" asked Gunther to the pilot.

"This damn engine has been giving me trouble all week," complained the pilot. "If we're going on a long journey, I just want to check it."

Gunther looked at his watch. "What's the problem?" he asked.

"The fuel line," said the pilot. "It's causing the engine to intermittently cut out."

"What?"

"To stop," said the pilot, clearly frustrated.

"How long before its fixed?" asked Gunther.

Fever

The pilot shrugged his shoulders.

"I don't know, forty minutes maybe a couple of hours…"

Gunther turned around to see that Karl had walked over himself to investigate. "What is this idiot saying?" he asked.

"He says the fuel line is leaking," replied Gunther.

"Did we pay for the plane to be ready?"

"Ya."

Karl raised his gun and shot the pilot in the head at point blank range. Gunther looked stunned.

"Stephan knows how to fly this thing," snapped Karl. "Get him to fix it and quickly."

Just as Karl killed the pilot, the shot echoed and boomed inside the hangar, waking Lisa. She looked around and saw Karl and Gunther along with the dead pilot, while the rest of the men, were pre-occupied with loading boxes. Slowly Lisa pulled herself up from the stretcher and hobbled to the back of the hangar, behind a plane.

At the back, she found an old doorway, with WWII army writing saying MUNITIONS STORE - NO SMOKING. The door opened and she went inside.

Fever

Karl looked at the stretcher, then at the back inside the hangar and saw that Lisa was gone.

"Shit," he said and ran back inside the hangar with Gunther. They looked behind the small plane at the back of the hangar and saw the door open into the old WWII store.

Gunther pulled out his gun from his backpack. Karl waved at him negatively.

"You know she's injured. She won't get far. Stay here. I'll get her. But get the plane ready to go!"

Gunther nodded as Karl entered the old munition tunnels.

******

Inside the helicopter, Anna the co-pilot pointed out the horizon.

"We're coming up on the airfield in a couple of minutes," she said. "Matt can cover you when you get off. But if they have heavy rounds, we've got to get out of there quick."

I understand, said Mitch. "Just get me as close as you can and I will be fine."

******

Inside the tunnels, Karl walked carefully through.

"Here Kitty, Kitty, Kitty. Here Kitty, Kitty, Kitty," he said.

In the pitch black, Lisa had found a space to hide. She could hear Karl walking closer towards her and then the light of the flash light.

****

Outside, Gunther looked at his watch as the final boxes of gold were loaded. "Start her up," he said, before pressing down on his two-way radio.

"We're ready, he said". But there was no answer from Karl, only static.

In the distance, the sound of helicopter blades could be heard coming closer.

"Shit," said Gunther as he pressed the two-way radio. "Karl. Get back here now. They're coming."

Still nothing but static. Gunther looked at the men.

"Whoever it is, hold them off, until I get the boss," he said, before turning around and running back in the direction of the tunnel entrance.

Fever

****

Inside the tunnels, Karl stopped and turned off the flash light.

"You know the funny thing Lisa," he said. "When you calm yourself down, you have time to remember you have other senses. Not just sight and hearing. But smell."

As he spoke, Karl reached out from the darkness and grabbed Lisa, who screamed.

"Calm down or I will knock you out," growled Karl.

He turned his flash light back on and walked Lisa back towards the exit from the tunnels and back into the old hangar.

****

The army helicopter landed in front of the Dash-8 as Mitch got out, holding a semi-automatic weapon, covered by Matt. But as soon as he had taken a few steps, the men behind the Dash-8 started firing in the direction of the helicopter, narrowly missing Mitch, but hitting Matt in the leg.

Mitch returned fire as Matt fired wildly, in agony, hitting Elias behind the plane. As Elias fell to the ground, his weapon fired rounds into the wing of the plane and in a second there was an almighty explosion, tearing the plan apart and sending a fireball into the old hangar.

Mitch was also flattened by the blast. When he picked himself up, he ran over to Matt, who had started to tie a tourniquet around his left calf, to stop the bleeding.

In-between Mitch and Matt and the damaged hangar was a thick black cloud of burning fuel and wreckage. Ewen and Anna sprinted over to join them, armed with semi-automatic weapons.

"I'm OK," said Matt. "Lets get these arseholes."

Chapter 13

Karl and Lisa had made it to the exit of the tunnels, when the fireball ripped into the hangar and Gunther was badly hurt by flying shrapnel.

As Gunther picked himself up and moved toward the front of the hangar, he came under fire from Ewen, Anna, Matt and Mitch.

Gunther limped back to Karl and Lisa and shook his head negatively. "I can't see how many there are," he said. "Our best bet is to go back in and see if we can pick off a few or to find another exit."

"I'm sorry my dear, but the planned holiday to Indonesia has been cancelled," smiled Karl. "Maybe our new arrivals can help with an alternate suggestion."

Gunther stepped back into the tunnels first, with Karl holding Lisa out front as a shield.

"I can't get a clean shot," yelled Ewen.

"Wait," yelled Mitch as he entered the hangar and briefly locked eyes with Lisa.

Ewen, Anna, Matt and Mitch watched, with their guns fixed as Karl, still using Lisa as a shield, disappeared into the tunnels.

Fever

****

Gunther and Karl holding Lisa move further into the tunnels. They come to a T- junction in the tunnel.

"Its a labyrinth."

Karl laughed and looked at Lisa. "Our lucky day."

They turned left and then turn right again into another tunnel.

****

Mitch inched forward, checking each corner, before he felt a tap on his shoulder. It was Matt.

"Is he going to try and shoot his way out?", asked Matt.

"Karl's not looking for a last stand. He's looking for a diversion to use to escape. Tell Ewen and Anna to stay outside.

Matt nodded and limped back.

****

Karl held Lisa tightly, while Gunther guarded their rear. They arrived at a door at the end of one of the tunnels. They pushed it open and moved inside.

"Your hurting my arm," complained Lisa.

"I'm sorry Lisa, but I don't think I can take your word, you won't run away."

"I promise," she said.

Karl turned to Gunther.

"Stay here. We'll look for an exit and then double back."

Gunther nodded as Karl and Lisa moved through the doorway to the next set of tunnels. Gunther stayed behind, checking for any people following.

Chapter 13

Chapter 14

Mitch moved quietly through the tunnels closer to where Gunther was hiding behind the door.

Just then, Gunther pushed his gun through and opened fire. Mitch ducked down and out of direct fire.

He reached down and pulled out a grenade. He pulled out the pin and held onto the catch. Mitch carefully moved over to the corner, put his arm around and started firing again. He moved slightly forward and threw the grenade with his uninjured arm toward the door. The grenade bounced twice and lodged just at the opening. At the explosion, Mitch rushed forward to the door and pushed it open.

****

Karl and Lisa pushed forward.

"These damn tunnels," cursed Karl. "There must be an exit."

"You'll never make it."

Karl shook her.

"Shut up, before I lose my temper."

Karl heard the explosion of the grenade. He looked back and focused on another door. On it was the faded word EXIT. He dragged Lisa back toward the door and tried to open it. It was jammed.

"Stand back."

As Karl leant over to put a grenade in front of the door to blow it, Lisa broke free of his grip and ran back towards the sound of the previous explosion. Karl turns to see her just turn the corner and out of sight.

"Damn you."

He got up and ran after her.

****

Mitch walked over carefully towards Gunther, lying on the ground, his gun was damaged and laying close to the side wall. Gunther was bleeding from a head wound. As he leant forward to prod Gunther with the butt of his gun, Gunther kicked him in the knee and then swept his right leg over and hook-kicked the gun from Mitch's hands. Mitch fell back in pain.

Gunther got up and pulled out a hunting knife, moving forward.

"We should have killed you in that miserable town."

Gunther lunged at Mitch. But Mitch grabbed Gunther's arm holding the blade and pushed it with all his might to hold it away from his chest. He grabbed

Gunther's other arm and held it back as well. They rolled over, still in a deadly embrace.

Gunther pushed the blade closer, and closer still. Mitch deflected the knife and it cut into Mitch's right shoulder. He yelled in pain and kneed Gunther in the groin. Gunther released his grip and as he did, Mitch leant over and picked up the gun he had dropped.

"Piss off."

He shot three bullets at Gunther, at almost point blank range, emptying the magazine.

As Gunther dropped to the ground dead, Lisa limped back into the room. She ran over to Mitch. Mitch put the gun down and hugged her, blood flowing from the knife wound to his shoulder.

"Are you all right?" he asked

"Fine," she said

"Let's go."

Just as Lisa helped steady Mitch to leave, Karl arrived.

"Leaving without me again Lisa?" smiled Karl. "Lisa step away from Mitch."

"It's over Karl," said Mitch.

"It's never really over. You know that."

Karl moved over to Lisa, grabbed her arm and threw her out of the way.

Chapter 14

"You certainly were a bundle of trouble old policeman," growled Karl.

Mitch said nothing, staring directly into Karl's eyes. "You promised not to harm him or me," shouted Lisa.

Karl looked around at Lisa. "Yes, well indeed I did."

Karl produced a grenade from his belt and pulled out the pin, while still holding the release mechanism.

"It will be this little device that bring our collective demise, won't it."

Instead of looking scared, Lisa was smiling. Karl was bemused and watched as Lisa unbuttoned her shirt to reveal the edge of her bra and a hint of her firm breasts.

"Isn't this what you've wanted all along?" she said.

Karl stared open mouthed at her.

"Say, it Karl. You want me, don't you?"

Karl moves away from Mitch lying semi conscious against the wall and towards Lisa.

"You have no idea, but frankly your timing sucks," said Karl. "However, before we go there is one last thing I do wish."

Karl moved to Lisa, embracing her while still holding the grenade in his hand. As he kissed her the grip on the gun in his other hand loosened.

Fever

Just then Mitch made a final lunge at Karl with a jagged piece of rusty iron. He thrust it with all his might into Karl's back.

Karl yelled in agony as Mitch twists the old piece of metal deeper through the rib cage of Karl. Lisa grabbed Karl's hand and held it tight, but as he fell the release mechanism flung off the grenade.

In an instant, Mitch retrieved the grenade and put it under the chest of Karl, before throwing himself and Lisa away flat to the floor as the grenade exploded.

As the smoke cleared, Mitch picked Lisa back up and hugged her.

****

Mitch, held the hand of Lisa on a stretcher as they loaded her onto a helicopter. He lent over to her as the rotors start to turn.

"You can be my partner anytime," he smiled.

"Is that a threat or a promise?" she coughed as the rotors increase in speed.

"I got a call from Perth," yelled Mitch against the noise of the helicopter. "They'll be cleaning up at Warratama for months. So if you need a break you know where you'll find me."

Chapter 14

Mitch leant over and kissed Lisa on the cheek before stepping away from the helicopter as it took off. Smiling, he turned and headed out into the blackness of the night.

www.ingramcontent.com/pod-product-compliance
Lightning Source LLC
Chambersburg PA
CBHW080822120626
46556CB00010B/3352